3J

COME MEET MUFFIN!

Joyce Carol Oates

Illustrated by Mark Graham

THE ECCO PRESS

THE ECCO PRESS
100 West Broad Street
Hopewell, New Jersey 08525

Published simultaneously in Canada by
Penguin Books Canada Ltd., Ontario
Printed in Hong Kong

Library of Congress Cataloging-in-Publication Data
Oates, Joyce Carol, 1938–
Come meet Muffin / Joyce Carol Oates ; illustrated by Mark Graham.—1st ed.
p.   cm.
Summary: In helping two fawns find their mother in the woods, Muffin
the brave cat becomes lost himself and must try to find his way home again.
ISBN 0-88001-556-X
[1. Cats—Fiction.   2. Deer—Fiction.   3. Lost children—Fiction.]   I. Graham,
Mark, 1952–   ill.   II. Title.
PZ7.01056Co   1998
[E]—dc21   97-43453

Designed by Mark Graham

The text of this book is set in Hiroshige

9 8 7 6 5 4 3 2

FIRST EDITION, 1998

For Lily

Muffin is a special kitty who came to live with the Smith family.

One day long ago, when Muffin was only a tiny kitten, he found himself lost on a country road. The Smith family was driving by in their car, and their little girl Lily saw him and cried, "Oh, look! A kitten!"

When the Smiths brought Muffin home, he was small enough to fit in the palm of a hand. The other cats in the family welcomed Muffin and made him feel at home.

Muffin was a gentle cat, but he was also very brave. One day, when a strange dog came into the Smiths' yard and began to chase Christabel, Muffin hurried in front of her so that the dog would chase him instead.

Muffin climbed up the tree so fast the dog could not figure out where Muffin had gone.

Muffin was also very protective, so he always slept at the foot of Lily's bed. Because he was so big and soft, he kept Lily's toes warm on winter nights.

One morning, Muffin heard a sound outside in the snow. He climbed up onto the windowsill and saw two fawns in the backyard! He sensed the fawns were lost because their mother was nowhere in sight. Muffin quickly squeezed out the window and ran to help the fawns. He remembered when he had been lost as a kitten. He knew the fawns wanted their mother.

Now when he got outside, Muffin looked for the fawns' hoof-prints in the snow. He followed the prints back towards the woods. The fawns were very shy—they had never seen a cat before! But this cat seemed to know where he was going, so they followed him as he stepped carefully through the snow. Muffin disliked getting his feet wet and cold, so he walked carefully in the hoofprints that had already been made.

It was a windy winter morning, but Muffin walked for miles.
He led the fawns across a field of tall grass stiffened to ice by
the cold. He took them to a frozen brook where, through the
ice, they could see golden fish darting and playing.

Finally, Muffin led the fawns into tall evergreen woods, where an owl with gorgeous plumage dozed overhead in a tree limb. All the birds sang in excitement that Muffin and the fawns were there.

It was in this part of the forest that Muffin at last found the fawns' mother. She was so happy to see them!

The fawns ran to their mother, and she kissed and groomed them. She thanked Muffin for his help and led her fawns away deeper into the woods.

Muffin had been so worried about the fawns that he had not realized how far he had come into the woods! He had never been so far from home. With the deer gone, the woods were very quiet and lonely. There were so many hoofprints in the snow that he didn't know which direction to take. Muffin tried to MEOW—but there was no one to hear him. He thought, "How can I find my way back home?"

Then he remembered—of course, he could climb a tree! Using his sharp claws, Muffin climbed the tallest evergreen in the woods. He surprised the sleeping owl with the gorgeous plumage, who blinked and stared, saying, "Whoooo—?" He woke up a family of squirrels, who were grumpy and scolded, "Tsk! Tsk! Tsk!" But it was the tiny chickadees who encouraged Muffin by chirping, "Tweeee, tweeee, tweeee!"

Muffin was as high up in the tree as the birds! He wasn't afraid, though, because he kept his claws sunk into the tree and held himself very still. The cold winter wind whistled through his whiskers and the bristly hairs in his ears, making tears come into his eyes. After looking through the swirling snow for some time, Muffin finally saw his house, miles away. He thought, "I was never lost, really. My house was always there."

Muffin climbed back down the tree and made his way out of the evergreen woods. He trotted back up the slippery long hill, across the frozen brook. He pranced through the field of tall grass turned to ice and into the backyard of his house. He was HAPPY to be home!

All the family was outside looking for Muffin. He had been gone for hours! Everyone was calling "Muffin? Muffin? Kitty-kitty-*kitty!*" and looking very worried. Little Lily was the most worried of all and had been biting her lip to keep from crying.

Little Lily saw Muffin first and cried, "Muffin! There's Muffin!" Everyone ran to meet him. Christabel, who missed Muffin very much, ran to him, too, purring and rubbing around him with her tail. Everyone was surprised— it was the first time pretty Christabel had ever kissed Muffin!

That day, Muffin was even allowed to eat at the kitchen table with the Smiths. He PURRED the loudest anyone had ever heard him PURR.

When Margaret came to visit Lily, the two girls held Muffin on their laps together—he was so big, he fit just right! To show how much he loved them, Muffin turned over onto his back, so they could rub his soft stomach. His PURR said, "I am the happiest cat in the world—and brave, too!"

GOLF
THE WOMAN'S GAME

ROGER VAUGHAN

Foreword by
NANCY LOPEZ

STEWART, TABORI & CHANG   NEW YORK

FOR KIPPY

Text copyright © 2000 by Roger Vaughan

Project editor: Sandra Gilbert
Production: Kim Tyner
Designer: Susi Oberhelman

Published in 2001 by
Stewart, Tabori & Chang
A division of Harry N. Abrams, Inc.
115 West 18th Street
New York, NY 10011

Library of Congress Cataloging-in-Publication Data

Vaughan, Roger.
Golf, the woman's game / Roger Vaughan ; foreword by Nancy Lopez.
p. cm.
ISBN 1-58479-063-6 (alk. paper)
1. Golf for women—United States—History.
2. Women golfers—United States—Biography. I. Title.

GV966 . V38 2001
796.352'08'0973—dc21

The text of this book was composed in Bembo,
captions were composed in Futura.

Printed and bound in Hong Kong.

10 9 8 7 6 5 4 3 2 1

FIRST PRINTING

CONTENTS

FOREWORD

I'VE BEEN PLAYING GOLF SINCE I COULD HOLD A CLUB, and I've been a professional for more than twenty years. Now I'm in the golf equipment business. My whole life has been consumed by golf, or more specifically, women's golf. But it took this book to make me fully realize what a rich and varied history we women golfers have established over the scant hundred or so years that golf has been played in this country.

Looking back at the constraints on women who wanted to play golf, it's a wonder golf ever sustained as a sport for women. But golf is a game that gets under your skin. I remember how it captured my whole being when I was a young girl. I ate, drank, and slept golf. I loved the excitement of winning even a pee wee tournament. I'd drift off to sleep at night amid visions of hitting balls, excited as a kid before Christmas at the prospect of playing again the next day.

But even as late as the 1960s, when I first realized I had a talent for the game, I wasn't exactly welcomed into the sport. I had to fight plenty of battles. First there were the all-male school teams that had to be opened up. Then there were country club restrictions on women. Some clubs still prohibit women from playing at all. But once golf hooks us, we *will* find a way to play. That's the spirit that Roger Vaughan has captured in this book.

He's assembled a great cast of characters. As much as I have played, I don't know a lot about the history of the woman's game. The stories the older players have to tell—stories I didn't know—brought a smile to my face.

Every day I see more and more women playing golf, and that gives me a great feeling. After reading this book, I realize how proud I am to be playing on the LPGA tour.

NANCY LOPEZ

INTRODUCTION

I TOOK UP GOLF WHEN I WAS TWELVE. I HAD FUN whacking balls and hanging around the country club with the other kids, caddying and playing. But it didn't last.

I didn't play again until five years ago. Since then I've had three lessons, one from a male professional, the other two from a female. There's no question I learned more from the woman. I mentioned this to her after the second lesson, and she explained that for women, golf has to be about rhythm and a smooth swing. Then she diplomatically advanced the notion that most male amateurs simply cannot aspire to hitting a ball 300-plus yards off the tee or hitting pitching wedges 160 yards like the male pros. Most male amateurs, she went on after checking to make sure my testosterone level had not been threatened, can more easily relate to the game as played by female professionals.

Instinct told me my lady teacher was right. But after writing this book, I'm not sure. Because now I know how many golfers on the Ladies Professional Golf Association Tour *average* more than 250 yards off the tee and regularly hit pitching wedges 130 yards. Not many male amateur golfers can relate to that, but those numbers are a bit more realistic. And that business about rhythm and a smooth swing is something all men could profit from if we could only stop trying to hit the ball 300 yards. The woman's approach to golf contains instructional value for those of us who dream of consistently breaking 90.

This book has been great fun to write. Sometimes people gave me quizzical looks when I told them what I was working on. I would simply explain that I love women and I love golf, so this project was right up my alley. I had the great fortune to spend time with Betsy Rawls, Louise Suggs, and Peggy Kirk

Bell. And I had wonderful conversations with legends like Carol Mann, Kathy Whitworth, Nancy Lopez, and Marilynn Smith, among many others.

While waiting to see Peggy Bell, I found an irresistible, slightly used seven-wood in a shop in Pinehurst, N. C. Peggy saw it in my car, and soon we were heading for the range with a bucket of balls. She chose a six-iron from her bag. In her mid-seventies, Peggy Bell has a swing that is still poetry in motion. She didn't hit the ball as far as she used to, a fact that had her grumbling to herself, but every ball ended up within the thirty-foot circle.

Perhaps the biggest kick for me was learning about Glenna Collett Vare, who ruled the links in the 1920s and is considered one of the greatest female golfers of all time. The fact that Vare was also a very good writer provides us with excellent insights into this determined and elegant woman who was so adept at promoting the game she loved.

My focus on the subject of women and golf inevitably came home with me. With all the golf talk in the house because of the book project, my wife, who has fond memories of playing as a teenager with her grandfather, took up the game again after not holding a club for thirty-five years. After two lessons, several sessions at the driving range, and a few hours on the lawn hitting practice balls, she was ranting and raving about what a frustrating game it was, how she wasn't learning anything, and how she was wasting her time. I listened to her with complete understanding. It had taken me three seasons before I was breaking 100.

But when my wife came home after her third lesson, she was calm, light-hearted, and couldn't wait to tell me how the last dozen balls she'd hit that day went long and straight. I surprised her later in the kitchen as she addressed an imaginary ball with an imaginary club in her hand. Unembarrassed, she began reciting the litany of chipping. Lately, I've noticed she's been buying golf "skorts." She loves the putter I got her for her birthday. And just a few days ago, she came by my office around 4 P.M. and asked if I felt like taking a break. I asked what she had in mind. And she said, innocently, "I thought we might go hit some balls."

ROGER VAUGHN, *Oxford, Maryland*

SOUTHAMPTON, NEW YORK Carved out of the gently rolling, scrub-covered sandy terrain of eastern Long Island, Shinnecock Hills Golf Club is one of the first eighteen-hole golf courses in the United States. Women were involved as both stockholders and players from Shinnecock's beginnings in 1891. The elegant clubhouse design by Stanford White bespeaks feminine influence. The first Women's National Amateur Championship (1895) was won by one of three Shinnecock members entered in that tournament.

SHINNECOCK HILLS

1 Hitting Things with Sticks

THOSE WHO HAVE RESEARCHED "COLF," AND "KOLF," golf's antecedents in the low countries of Europe (c. 1300), and the beginnings of the game as we know it in Scotland (c. 1450), have concluded that golf is a natural progression of the fact that the male of our species has always enjoyed hitting things with a stick. Primitive man was a hunter, a role that often required hitting four- and two-legged "things" with a stick, employing accuracy, timing, considerable strength, and a penchant for violence. So when it came to making a game of that deadly craft, women were not included. Our female ancestors were gatherers, a role that did not often include hitting things with sticks other than pesky dogs and unruly children. When the lives of homo sapiens did allow for sport, the elements of strength and killer instinct prevailed. To this day, in many games where sticks are employed, there is a distinct carryover from the days when the object of the hunt had fur. Until the last fifty years, stick games have held no place for women.

Golf has always been different. Golf is the only stick sport where the object that one hits is not in motion. That changes everything. The pace of golf is slow. Golfers do not run, fake, cut, repeatedly stop and start, or engage in physical struggles with other players. For that reason, golfers don't need protective padding, helmets, or aerobic conditioning. Another unique aspect of golf is that every player has a personal "thing," in this case a ball, to hit. And every player has a variety of sticks from which to choose. The atmosphere on the golf playing field—the links, or course—is relaxed. A player dressed in clothes that would not look terribly out of place on the street walks sedately to where the ball is located, studies the situation, and selects a stick. Those watching observe the sport's

The quintessential woman golfer of 1892 at Shinnecock Hills: immaculately dressed, wedding band in place, club in hand, resolute.

15

unique rules of etiquette and remain quiet as mice while the player hits the ball. Golf is fiercely competitive, but only in the sense that individual efforts are compared and ranked at the conclusion of play. Golf is more a test of concentration and finesse than strength and killer instinct—although the games of many male players continue to suffer from those persistent, primitive hominid traits.

From its beginnings, golf has attracted women. It involves exercise, a long walk in pleasant surroundings. It offers relaxation, promises a certain kind of reverie. Jerome Travers, four-time winner of the Men's National Amateur Championship in the 1920s, once waxed alliterative about the joys of golf, writing about "the melody of the mid-iron; the music of the mashie; the poetry of the putter; the drone of the driver; the tempo of the tee." Women could play golf, and they did play, even though it took their male counterparts some time to get used to the idea that it was okay for ladies to hit things with sticks.

Mary, Queen of Scots, is without a doubt the most famous, first-of-the-female golfers. She played in the mid-1500s. Queen Mary is credited with introducing the term and concept of "caddie" to the sport. She had brought sons of French noblemen to Scotland to serve as pages in her court. She regularly took these "cadets" with her to the golf course. They may or may not have carried her clubs, looked for lost balls, and performed other chores assigned to today's caddies. Such information isn't available. But since "cadet" evolved into "caddie," one must assume that these young lads were in some way useful to the Queen in her forays on the fairways.

The story was circulated that Her Highness was seen playing with a male companion not long after her husband (and cousin) Lord Darnley had been strangled in the garden of their home, which subsequently had been blown up. That the Queen probably knew about the plot to kill Darnley and that her partner on the links was one James Hepburn, Fourth Earl of Bothwell, whom she'd been seeing and eventually married, added to the scandal. Robert Browning, editor of Britain's *Golfing* magazine from 1910 to 1955, and whose *A History of Golf* is perhaps the best scholarly work on the sport, discounts such vicious gossip. But

An artist's rendition of Mary, Queen of Scots, playing golf with Lord Chastelard at St. Andrews in 1563. Her "cadets" (caddies) are at right.

there is plenty of evidence that the high-spirited Queen Mary did play the game in between hatching royal plots, quelling insurrections, leading armies, escaping from an island where she was held captive, and finally being beheaded by Queen Elizabeth I. Perhaps golf is how this busy woman relaxed.

Browning unearthed another woman who influenced golf in the early days. In the beginning of the 1800s, an English Dame by the name of Margaret Ross was thought to be a witch. Browning wrote, "It was seriously believed of her that she carried political animosity to the length of interfering with her opponents' games of golf. She used her unholy powers to convert herself into the golf ball they were playing and spoiled their game by deliberately rolling out of line on the putting green or hopping with malice aforethought into the deepest depths of a hazard."

Dame Margaret Ross could also apparently bring about positive results. Apparently she used her powers to gain a seat in Parliament for Sir Patrick Murray once he agreed to vote her way. To keep her insider on the hook, she improved his golf game as well.

Musselburgh and Inveresk, twin towns in Scotland, became hot spots in women's golf in the 1700s. Gorgeous golf links lined both banks of the Esk River, which ran between the towns. Just as mountain children learned alpine skills, the children of Musselburgh and Inveresk learned golf. The members of the Royal Musselburgh Golf Club began playing an annual tournament for a silver cup in 1774. According to old records, the women of the area also played. Given that some of the trophies awarded included creels and small fish baskets, the women playing were probably employed in the town's fishing industry. The golfing interest of blue-collar workers was a unique departure from the otherwise elitist nature of the game. According to one statistical report of the day, "As the women do the work of men . . . their strength and activity is equal to their work. Their amusements are of the masculine kind. On holidays they frequently play at golf, and on Shrove Tuesday there is a standing match at football between the married and the unmarried women, in which the former are always victors."

It wasn't until the mid-1800s that golf was officially recognized in Europe as a socially acceptable game for women. Typically, and still true today, women would first swing a club at the suggestion of a father or brother. The first women's club, St. Andrews Ladies Golf Club, was founded in 1867, 250 years after the men's club of the same name. By 1874, there were seven clubs for women in Europe, including one at Musselburgh. The European Ladies' Golf Union was not formed until 1893, the year the first women's championship was held. As Browning wrote, "The pioneers of the ladies' championship had to put up with a good many gibes from self-sufficient males who were sure that the women would prove quite incompetent to run a championship or anything else." The tournament was, by all accounts, a great success, and it gave women's golf a jump-start in Europe.

The first issue of the British journal *Ladies Golf* contained an article that put golf in a most intriguing perspective: "Golf is a factor of no small importance in the mental, as well as the physical development of the modern girl. Before the era of golf the recreations of girlhood were practically restricted to croquet, and later to lawn tennis; only a fortunate minority were permitted to go in for horseback riding, clad in dangerous, flowing garments, and seated on sleek and ambling steeds discarded by their fathers.

Married women were even less happy. The store room, the kitchen, and the nursery supplied not only their serious occupation, but also their relaxation. This 'daily round,' lasting all day every day, produced a dullness of spirits that, while it shortened life, made it also less pleasant . . . None of the pre-golf pastimes led their devotees far afield or brought them together in such numbers as golf has done."

The ladies' putting green at St. Andrews, Scotland. Because of the rolling nature of the terrain, the green is known as "The Himalayas."

Golf arrived in the United States in the late 1800s. Historians generally acknowledge a gentleman named John Reid as being the Father of American golf. Reid grew up in Scotland and had watched golf evolve, but never played himself. He immigrated to Manhattan, where he became an executive in an iron-work. In 1888, he returned from a trip to Scotland with a set of golf clubs and demonstrated the game for friends on a field near his home. Holes were hastily scooped out of the ground with one of the clubs. Despite the makeshift links, all present were excited by the potential of the new sport, and at a dinner at Reid's home on November 14, 1888, the first golf club in the United States was founded. It was called St. Andrews, after Scotland's famous course. It was located in Yonkers, N.Y. John Reid was named president. The clubhouse was a tent.

Given the snail's pace of communication in the late 1800s, William Vanderbilt and two friends from Southampton, Long Island, had no idea that John Reid's St. Andrews Golf Club was up and running when they witnessed their first golf shots in the winter of 1890–1891 at a spa in Biarritz, France. Like other wealthy Americans of the day, Vanderbilt and friends had cottages in Europe, where they were always on the lookout for new amusements. Willie Dunn, who was part of a famous Scottish golfing family, was laying out an eighteen-hole course at Biarritz when he met the three Americans. No doubt Dunn smelled the money as he expressed his willingness to give them a demonstration. The wily Scot teed up several balls and chipped them onto a green 125 yards away. Some of them, Dunn later reported with pride, were quite close to the flag. The Americans were mightily impressed. "Gentlemen, this beats rifle shooting for distance and accuracy," Vanderbilt pronounced. "It's a game I think would go well in [America]." And that is how the Shinnecock Hills Golf Club, Southampton, N.Y., was conceived, according to a history of the club adapted by George Peper.

Golf balls were plunking down on American greenery from all directions. At about the same time the Southampton men were returning from France, a young French woman named Florence Boit was bringing the game to the Boston area. She and Vanderbilt could have been passengers on the same

trans-Atlantic crossing. In 1892, Boit brought her clubs along when she visited her uncle, Arthur Hunnewell, in Wellesley, Mass. She assumed that golf was being played in New England in those days. When she discovered that was not the case, Boit demonstrated the game to her uncle's friends and subsequently supervised the building of several seven-hole pitch-and-putt courses on neighboring lawns. Boit's introduction of the new game was said to be the hit of the season and stirred up a lot of interest in the Boston area.

One of those introduced to the game by Boit was Laurence Curtis. He persuaded the Country Club in Brookline, Mass., founded in 1881 around bowling, lawn tennis, and horse racing, to lay out a golf course on its grounds. Despite initial territorial rows between the golfers and the horsemen over the issue of hoofprints and other horse-related evidence on the greens, the country club purchased twenty sheep to keep the grass trimmed and voted to keep golf as an official sport.

Back in Southampton, Vanderbilt and friends were so enthusiastic about their discovery that they brought in a course designer from Scotland before general approval by the community was granted. But they needn't have worried. They began a subscription drive, and with money pouring in, hired one of the most popular young architects of the day, Stanford White, to design a clubhouse. Founded in 1891, by 1892 Shinnecock Hills Golf Club could rightly claim to be the first, or perhaps the second eighteen-hole course in America (the Chicago Golf Club also makes that claim); the first incorporated golf club; and the first to have a clubhouse.

Six women were among Shinnecock's original forty-four stockholding members. Peper wrote, "The women made their presence felt early. In September (1891), the ladies of the colony (Southampton) ordered a bough house to be erected on the spot where the clubhouse now stands and a golf rally, in the form of an afternoon tea, was given."

Shinnecock was the first club to include women on an equal footing, but equality wasn't always practiced. Newspaper reports of the day intimate that sexism was afoot at Shinnecock. One such piece in the *New York Herald* of 1891 reads in part, "If [the men] dared they would probably exclude women from the links . . . but they have resorted instead to the compromise of introducing ladies links adjoining their own, in which their sisters, wives, and sweethearts may disport themselves . . . without disturbing the lords of creation." But in fact it was the ladies rather than the lords of creation who were the movers and shakers behind the nine-hole Red course that was built for the women's exclusive use. It was seen as a training course that women—and only women—would have

Dressed in the proper golfing attire of the day, eight female members of Shinnecock Hills pose in front of the clubhouse in 1893.

to play three times within a set number of strokes in order to qualify for the long course. (In Europe, to this day, no player is allowed on many courses until he or she proves basic skills, and knowledge of the rules.) As one might imagine, and as Peper reported, "This distinction created a certain amount of dissatisfaction . . . In short time the two-course arrangement was abandoned in favor of a single, eighteen-hole layout."

David Goddard, a golfer who teaches sociology at John Jay College (City University of New York), is writing a complete history of Shinnecock. The women's early involvement in the club's beginnings is of particular interest to him. "Arguably," he writes in this work-in-progress, "the emphasis on women reflected that for the club to be a success it needed their support." He goes on to point out that social life in Southampton in the 1890s was clustered around one generic club, a church, and a bathing club, all located close to the village. The Shinnecock Club was three miles down the road—a fair jaunt in 1890. And while the course has rough-hewn natural beauty, it lacks the pure spectacle of California's ocean courses, or the overgrown, shade-dappled richness of southeastern courses. Shinnecock's course is laid out amid hardy grasses and wildflowers that flourish in sandy soil. It can be a bleak place. Low clouds off the nearby Atlantic Ocean often roll through, creating a damp chill even in mid-summer.

Without a clubhouse there would be little social life, and hence, little attraction for and support from women. Goddard writes, "Shinnecock might well have become a small male domain on the Hills . . . a new, Eveless Eden. . . . Thankfully, nothing of the sort happened, and the founders had the good sense to tell Stanford White they wanted a comfortable clubhouse with a ballroom and quarters for women as well as for men." Goddard concludes, "A new club and a practically unknown game required for its success the active involvement and participation of women." And their participation meant more than pouring tea.

Throughout America in the late 1800s, women's involvement in sports was growing at a remarkable rate. Southampton was in the vanguard of this movement. The fashionable Long Island summer colony has always been a mecca of

Students from
Wellesley College
in Wellesley, Mass.
taking golf lessons
on a campus
green in 1905.

sports activity for well-to-do young men *and* women. Brothers and sisters together sailed, swam, rode bicycles and horses, played polo, tennis, softball and even baseball. When golf came along, they were eager to add it to their sporting agendas.

Not only were women part of the scene at Shinnecock from the club's inception, they far outshone the men when it came to national competition. That had to be a bitter pill for the men. Equal opportunity was one thing. Superior skill (and flaunting it) was another matter. But women golfers' success

did not come easily in the 1890s. Men, in general, weren't enthusiastic about women taking up golf. From the outset, men tried to stake a claim on this new game and looked fondly upon the links as a refuge from both business and domestic stress. Golf became an acronym for Gentleman Only Ladies Forbidden.

In addition to fending off female interest in the sport, the male golfer's lot was complicated by the derision cast upon them by non-golfing males. Those self-styled macho individuals chortled at the idea of chasing a little white ball across a ten-acre lot with a stick, roundly dismissing golf as a game for sissies. So the male golfers were catching it from within their gender as well as from without. As one early male golfer lamented, "the tongue of America is sharp in its assault of those things which do not strike its fancy."

The tenor of the times was reflected by Ruth Underhill, the National Amateur Champion in 1899, who made her plea in a large, rare volume called *The Book of Sport*: "[Women] ought not to be turned off the courses en masse on certain days, as many of the men would like to have done; but, instead, a certain grade of play on the women's part might be made a basis for their admission."

The Shinnecock women wasted no time proving women deserved the consideration Ruth Underhill was promoting. In 1895, as Shinnecock's lone entry in the first Men's National Amateur Championship at Newport, R.I., was being defeated in the first round, a Shinnecock woman golfer was winning the first Women's National Amateur Championship at the Meadowbrook Golf Club in Hempstead, N.Y. In fact, three of the thirteen entries at Meadowbrook were women from Shinnecock. The winner, Mrs. Charles S. Brown, scored 11 on the first hole, and finished with 132 for the eighteen holes. Her card for the final six holes read, 4, 5, 7, 9, 14, 6. She won the tournament by two strokes.

It's tempting to be amused by Mrs. Brown's score. Even today's duffers might chuckle. But at the time, fewer than 100 women were playing golf in the United States. And Meadowbrook was the longest, most difficult course in the country with no special tee box for ladies. Other than the Scottish professionals, only a few men could break 100 at Meadowbrook in 1895.

Miss Lillian B. Hyde tees off at the Women's Metro-politan Golf Championship in West Orange, N.J. in May, 1914.

The clubs and balls were primitive, of course, and for the women, there was the matter of clothing—a whole lot of it. In her book, *Lesser Lives*, Diane Johnson lists the following items of *underwear* required (into the early 1900s) for the well-dressed Victorian lady: camisole, chemise, corset, six petticoats, stockings, and garters. This substantial foundation was topped by a long-sleeved, high-necked blouse, a full skirt belted at the waist, a multi-buttoned jacket, a hat, and (in the late 1800s), frequently a bustle. And of course, high-buttoned shoes. Now that you're dressed, Miss, here's your golf club. Give it a good full swing. Try not to split any seams. Ask a woman golfer of the 1890s her handicap, and she might have answered, my wardrobe.

Even playing under such a weight of clothing, women improved rapidly. Mrs. Arthur Turner, one of the three Shinnecock ladies in the Women's National Amateur Tournament in 1895, shot 155. As an indicator of how steep the learning curve was, Mrs. Turner took a whopping fifty strokes off her score the following year.

As extraordinary as Mrs. Turner's achievement was, it could not overshadow the play of another Shinnecock woman named Beatrix Hoyt, who won the second Women's National Amateur in 1896 at the age of sixteen. (She held the distinction of being the youngest ever to win the National Amateur until Laura Baugh's victory in 1971 when Baugh was a few months younger.) Hoyt won with a score of 95, bettering the previous year's winning round by thirty-seven strokes. Granddaughter of Salmon P. Chase, Abraham Lincoln's Secretary of the Treasury, Hoyt was said to have a low, round swing and a most enviable follow through. She repeated her championship win in 1897 and 1898. In 1899, she lost in the first round to a Mrs. Caleb Fox of Philadelphia (see pg. 30). In 1900, Hoyt was a medalist for the fifth straight year, but lost in the semi-final round in a sudden death playoff. At that point, at the age of twenty, Miss Hoyt retired from competition.

In this year 2000 women are active participants in all aspects of life—from politics to sports to the corporate hierarchy. But one can only imagine the combination of desire and aplomb it took for a woman of the 1890s to venture

Beatrix Hoyt (left), who won her first National Amateur Championship at age sixteen, during a match at Shinnecock Hills, her home club.

out on a golf course, clubs in hand. She had to ignore so many constraints of etiquette and behavior. Imagine the catty gossip that trailed her. To play golf, a person has to be willing to step into a solitary spotlight. When a player prepares to hit a ball, all activity and conversation in the vicinity stop. In the silence, the player is fully scrutinized as he or she addresses the ball and swings. Anyone who has ever taken a full swing at a golf ball and missed completely knows what it means to feel totally foolish. To put themselves in that tenuous position, the women of the 1890s who went out to play this difficult, frustrating game wore their courage on the puffy sleeves of their blouses. They were pioneers in the truest sense: trailblazers, and (literally) groundbreakers. Others took their lead, and proficiency increased. In the Women's National Amateur just sixteen years later (1923), the winner shot an 84, with six other women breaking 90.

SHOOTING AT HER AGE

"Grandmother whangs the ball 200 yards from the tee right down the middle, lays them cold and dead on her approaches, and putts like a wizard."

THUS WAS MRS. CALEB FOX of Philadelphia (at right) described by a newspaper writer of the early 1920s. If only golf had come to America when Mrs. Fox was a girl, her name surely would have been even more prominent among women golfers of the early twentieth century. As it was, Mrs. Fox—a prominent society matron—was thirty years old in 1895 when the first National Amateur Championship was held. In 1899, she was a finalist in that tournament. She went on to win the Philadelphia National Championship five times (1907, 1908, 1910, 1911, and 1917).

When she died in 1928 at the age of sixty-seven, the *New York Times* published an obituary that praised her game: "Throughout her years of golfing [Mrs. Fox] depended largely upon her deadly putting and excellent approach shots to underscore an opponent. Her driving was good, but once near the green she played with unfailing precision, frequently holing out 12- to 15-foot putts to win in a crucial match. . . . Young players looked to her as an eager and infallible counselor in the ways of the game."

Mrs. Fox's most notable victory was her defeat of then National Champion, Glenna Collett, in 1923 when Mrs. Fox was sixty-two years old. She gave away forty-two years to the champion as she defeated her 2 and 1 in the final round for the title. Collett, who eventually won a record six National Championships and who would be widely acknowledged as one of the greatest women golfers ever to play the game, regularly outdistanced Mrs. Fox off the tees. That wasn't enough to overcome Fox's remarkable approach shots and putting.

Collett, who was typically gracious in defeat, later wrote about Mrs. Fox, calling her "the most heroic figure of all golfing history." Collett pointed out that Fox qualified for the 1925 Women's National with a score of 88. "Where are the men," Collett mused, "of three score and ten who will shoot an 88 with no putts conceded?"

Mrs. Fox had ten grandchildren. She didn't start to play golf until after she had raised her family.

When she was sixty-six, Mrs. Fox scoffed at the likes of afternoon naps and knitting. "None of it for me," she said, "as long as I can frolic through eighteen holes of golf and top it off with a practice session on the side."

One newspaper story about Mrs. Fox in the 1920s was headlined, "Wonder Woman of the Links," and spoke of more than her golf game. "There is that about Mrs. Fox that makes her honored . . . even loved by everyone with whom she comes in contact.. . . A player possessing a fine assortment of shots, one who serves the game, and with a personality that radiates sunshine are factors blending into such a wondrous character of the links as is Mrs. Fox."

PEBBLE BEACH, CALIFORNIA The Cypress Point Club is generally acknowledged as one of the most beautiful and challenging courses ever built. The course is situated on a spectacular section of coastline where Pacific Ocean rollers break against cliffs. Marion Hollins, the 1921 National Woman's Amateur Champion, was Cypress Point's founder and driving force. She optioned the land, hired legendary architect Alister MacKenzie, and personally envisioned the famous sixteenth hole: From the tee, the golfer must hit over the ocean to the green.

CYPRESS POINT

② THE EMANCIPATORS

William D. Richardson lauded the remarkable progress women had made in golf. "Only a few years ago, women's golf was confined to a narrow strip of country along the Atlantic seaboard. Today every section of the United States has its fair devotees of the royal and ancient pastime. Women's golf flourishes from coast to coast, and from the Gulf to the Great Lakes. Women now have their own associations, their own tournaments, and their doings on the links today command as much attention as those of men."

One might say that Richardson was just a tad over the top. But reading further, one discovers that Richardson's long and flattering opening is a setup for his more smug purpose, that of comparing female golfers to their male counterparts. "Are the leading women golfers today the equal of the leading men?" he asks, a few lines deeper into his story. One doesn't need to be a feminist to spot this rooster preparing to strut his stuff among the hens.

But one thing is clear: if women hadn't taken such mammoth strides on the golf course, showing what impressive scores could be registered using finesse, concentration, balance, sound tactical judgment, and athletic prowess, the need to compare their game head-to-head with the men's would never have come up—even as a way to establish that the best women golfers still didn't have enough strength and killer instinct to beat the best men.

Golf had taken off in the United States by 1925. According to the earliest records of the National Golf Foundation, there were 5,691 golf "facilities" in the United States by 1930. The overlapping grip used by Harry Vardon in 1900

Joyce Wethered, the queen of British Golf, playing her first golf match in America at Glenhead, Long Island, in May, 1935.

THE
LADIES'
HOME
JOURNAL

NOVEMBER 1909
FIFTEEN CENTS

PAINTED BY HARRISON FISHER
THE CURTIS PUBLISHING COMPANY, PHILADELPHIA

Life

*Distance Lends
Enchantment*

had become standard. And by 1925, men's college golf teams had been around
twenty-five years, with Harvard, Yale, and Princeton leading the way. Spurred by
necessity and frustration, technology had advanced the golf ball from a hand-
sewn leather sack of compressed feathers to a lively, rubber-cored ball wound
with elastic. Invented by bicycle maker Coburn Haskell as a way to lengthen his
own game, the cover of the revolutionary ball that bore his name was complete
with dimples. Clubs had also improved. The heretofore curved faces of irons
were flattened and pitched deeper for more loft, with grooves added to induce
backspin. Woods were made of the more dense persimmon wood for improved

impact. The golf tee—a small wonder—had been invented. And golf stars like Francis Ouimet, the first amateur to win the U.S. Open, were standing tall beside their all-star contemporaries in more established sports.

The women golfers of America were working hard to keep pace with their British counterparts. In 1912, a hard-hitting Brit named Cecil Leitch won the first of the twelve national titles she would accumulate by 1926. She attacked the ball off the tees with a vengeance, hitting powerful, low-trajectory shots typical of only the best men. So dominant was Miss Leitch that in one Canadian Open she was fourteen holes up halfway through the thirty-six-hole final. Leitch has been called the emancipator of women's golf in Great Britain.

Joyce Wethered took up where Leitch left off. The then-unknown Wethered beat Leitch in the 1920 English Ladies Amateur Championship and went on to win it the next three years. Wethered was a six-foot tall, slender woman who had begun playing golf on holidays as a youngster after her family purchased a vacation house in Scotland adjacent to a golf course. She and her older brother, Roger, played every day and kept charts of their progress. Roger went on to be the captain of the Oxford golf team and win the British Amateur in 1923. Roger urged his sister to begin playing competitive golf when she was nineteen. Years later, Joyce would become the queen of British golf.

According to witnesses, the smooth, easy sweep of Joyce Wethered's swing made the difficult sport seem effortless. She understood the importance of leading the club head with a rotation of the hips. Wethered also worked on the inner game, the all-important mental side of golf. Her powers of concentration were renowned. Many years before it became popular sports wizardry, she was visualizing her shot as she addressed the ball. Her accuracy was phenomenal. A shy person, Wethered's demeanor on the course was cool and unemotional. The great Bobby Jones called her the best golfer he had ever seen—man or woman.

Back in America, a number of women golfers were establishing their own illustrious niches in golf, providing inspirational examples for women across the nation who were becoming intrigued by the game. At the time, trial and error was much more available than professional instruction. And there was something to be said for the long-term value of learning by experience. Harriot and Margaret Curtis believed in this concept. Each won a U.S. Women's Amateur Championship (1906 and 1907, respectively). But the sisters are best remembered for their efforts to initiate friendly competition between United States and British women's teams in what came to be known as the Curtis Cup.

If Joyce Wethered was the emancipator of women's golf in Great Britain, Alexa Stirling played that role in the United States. Stirling grew up in suburban Atlanta, Ga., with a golf course nearby. A young fellow named Bobby Jones was her neighbor. There's a story that Alexa, age twelve, beat Bobby, age

From left to right, Britain's Cecil Leitch (1923) and America's Harriot Curtis and her sister Margaret (1915) show their form on the tee.

six, in a six-hole tournament that was part of a neighborhood children's party, making her the only woman ever to beat the man who would become a legendary champion. It was no fluke. This slight, freckled redhead would become the first American woman golfer to draw world acclaim for the quality of her play. She won three successive National Amateur Championships (1916—with a pause for the war years—1919, and 1920), and was a finalist in three others. In 1925 her medal (best qualifying) score was a record 77. Her approach to the game was businesslike. Her form was exceptional. And her philosophy bolstered the confidence of women golfers everywhere: "The player who is going to win most often," Stirling wrote, "is not the one who is superior in strength of distance, but the one who can make the fewest mistakes and keep out of as much trouble as possible, but when once in trouble can cope with any situation."

When it came to coping with situations, it was hard to find someone with more and varied talents than Marion Hollins. Another U.S. Women's Amateur winner (1921), Hollins was also captain of the first Curtis Cup team. She was an excellent polo player, skilled at driving a coach and four on city streets, a steeplechase rider, and among the first women to race automobiles in competition. But the extraordinary Miss Hollins is best remembered for her work in breaking the gender barriers that had been erected between women and a game they were fast growing to love. Men were doing what they could to control the courses and the clubs. In some cases, wives and daughters were allowed to be associate members of their husband's and father's golf clubs. Divorce (or death of a husband) unfailingly terminated that arrangement. Single women weren't allowed on most courses. Based on the argument that because of their jobs men were only free to play on weekends, women's play was often restricted to weekdays. Other issues ranged from the lack of women's locker rooms to limited clubhouse use. And when golf courses were designed, women were rarely even considered, let alone consulted. All the courses were generally too long for most women's games. There were no ladies tees at the time to ameliorate that problem.

Marion Hollins realized that women needed their own golf courses, and

Atlanta's Alexa Stirling at the 1920 Women's National Amateur Championship which she won for the third time in a row.

Marion Hollins tees
off at Pebble Beach's
seventh hole (left).
On the beach at
Cypress Point (right),
Hollins stands on the
site of the first green.
The eighteenth green
at Pasatiempo in
1930 (opposite). On
the course she helped
Alister MacKenzie
design, Marion Hollins
scored a hole-in-one
on this green.

she had the vision, determination, and the financial means to build them. Her father had been a partner of J. P. Morgan. He went broke after leaving Morgan to start a business of his own. But as David Outerbridge reported in his 1998 biography of Marion Hollins's *Woman in a Man's World*, she made a considerable fortune of her own in oil by speculating against the odds. Hollins didn't wait long to put the money to good use. She helped found and finance The Women's National Golf and Country Club on Long Island (now the Glen Head Country Club), one of the first clubs for women. Then she moved to California and built two courses: Pasatiempo in Santa Cruz, and ocean-fronted Cypress Point on the Monterey Peninsula. The latter, with its fairways weaving along the spectacular, surf-pounded, rocky coast, is often referred to as the Sistine Chapel of golf. Both were designed by Alister MacKenzie, who carried out Marion Hollins' ideas. Many were the days Hollins's would hit ball after ball, with MacKenzie watching, to determine the proper placement of greens. (MacKenzie would later team up with Bobby Jones to build the famed Augusta National Golf Club in Georgia.)

With the barriers being slowly dismantled, women focused on playing competitive golf. And when it came to serious golf, one name surpasses all others in the 1920s and 1930s: Glenna Collett. Like so many of the accomplished early golfers, Collett came from a family of means. And in the 1920s, leisure time—which golf requires in considerable amounts—was a luxury of the rich.

When Glenna Collett's parents found themselves with a budding athlete

on their hands, they worked hard to divert her attention from baseball, a sport at which she excelled. Croquet or riding were so much more suitable for young ladies. To please her mother, Glenna learned tennis and learned it well. Then her father, a champion cyclist, suggested golf to his daughter. It wasn't quite as dignified as tennis in those days, but when she began playing at age fourteen, she displayed natural abilities for the game. Collett was inspired to put in the hard work of mastering golf by the example of Alexa Stirling, who had won her own first Women's National as a teenager. "I succumbed to her influence the moment I saw her play," Collett wrote of Stirling in her autobiography, *Ladies in the Rough*. When Collett won her second Women's National in 1925, the woman she beat in the finals was Alexa Stirling. It was typical of Collett to downplay her victory. "The final round was 36 holes, and the result depended largely on stamina. Alexa was quite tired . . . and for that reason I was able to win quite easily."

When she began playing competitive golf, Collett was full of promise, but she suffered a crisis of confidence under the overwhelming pressure of tournament play. That changed in 1921, when she met Cecil Leitch in a tournament in Philadelphia. Assuming she had little hope of beating the famed British golfer, Collett tried a more focused strategy. She played to halve, or equal, her opponent's strokes hole by hole instead of trying to hit big, winning shots. It worked. The two began the eighteenth hole all even. Collett sank a ten-foot putt to win the match. From then on, Collett had the confidence to support her shot-making ability.

A young woman the media thought epitomized the American Girl, Glenna Collett helped further the emancipation of women's golf. A modest person, her manners were polished. She was both businesslike and gracious, traits that helped her deal with the bothersome publicity her accomplishments generated. Writing in *Collier's* magazine in 1930, Grantland Rice recounted an incident he had witnessed at Pinehurst Golf Club in 1922. A number of women were discussing Cecil Leitch's game. Collett stood at the edge of the group, silent and listening. Finally someone turned to her and asked, "'Glenna, have you ever seen Cecil Leitch play?' 'Yes,' she said, 'I've seen her.' Just that—nothing more.

Glenna Collett, who won a record six Women's National Amateur Championships, playing a match at Cypress Point in the 1920s.

Naturally someone promptly declared that Glenna had played against and had beaten Cecil Leitch, but at this point the young star faded from the scene. She had no liking whatsoever for public praise or discussion of her own skill."

Using clubs with hickory shafts, Collett was capable of driving more than 300 yards off the tee. One wonders how far she would have hit a modern, liquid-core golf ball covered with hundreds of aerodynamically shaped dimples, with a graphite-shafted, oversized titanium driver. With her enviable game and her dignified presence, Glenna Collett helped open country club doors to women and reflected media attention on other deserving lady golfers of the day.

Collett won the first of her record six Women's National titles in 1922. When she didn't make the finals in 1924, she was still the first woman ever to break 80 for eighteen holes. Collett was the tournament medalist that year with a 79. As an indicator of women's overall progress, five players were within six strokes of Collett. The National title escaped Collett's grasp in 1924, but it was the only tournament she entered that she didn't win. Her 1924 record of fifty-nine wins, one loss, is extraordinary for any year.

Collett went on to win the National title in 1925, 1928, 1929, and 1930. She got married in 1931, had two children, and took some time off the golf course. Then in perhaps her most rewarding—and her last—National Amateur win, she came out of her brief retirement at the age of forty-two and beat the eighteen-year-old sensation, Patty Berg, 3 and 2. Collett had to sink a long, difficult putt on the thirty-fourth hole to fight off Berg's valiant comeback.

Collett's nemesis was the mighty Joyce Wethered. She never beat Wethered in tournament play. Collett wrote about one British Ladies' Championship in which she met the British phenomenon. "I played as perfect a round as I'll ever play, I guess, although I topped two tee shots and hit two approach shots into bunkers. Each mistake cost me a hole. Miss Wethered was never in the rough, and never did she need more than two putts. She was over par on one hole, but had six birdies, four of them in a row."

It would have dismayed the late Green Bay Packer coach, Vince Lombardi, to know that winning was not the only thing for Collett. Those who think the obsession with winning is a modern-day competitive phenomenon should consider this sentiment expressed in 1930 by the late dean of sportswriters, Grantland Rice: "This is a day and age when most champions are supposed to be of the aggressive, 'killer type.' The competition is so keen that only grim determination and concentration can bring out victory. If there is one ounce of the killer in Glenna Collett's makeup, she has kept it carefully hidden. On the other hand, her sympathy for a losing opponent has cost her more than one match. Sport to her, even championship play, isn't quite that vital and important. . . . There is none of the grimness in her golf that one so often sees now among the best men and women players, amateur or professional. . . . She is one of the few who, in generously congratulating a winning opponent, seems actually to mean every word she says."

Rice wrote that Collett would never do anything—psychologically or otherwise—to adversely affect an opponent's play. "She wants to win, but not badly enough to go beyond her own skill for the day at winning." Rice quoted Collett: "I play golf largely for the fun and the exercise I get from it. I know how important concentration on every stroke is . . . but there is no fun in concentrating for three hours. That means nothing but hard work. If I tried to concentrate correctly on every stroke, I might play better golf. But I wouldn't get as much fun out of the game." One can imagine the ears of a thousand women golf aspirants happily perking up at that relaxed view of the game from their champion.

Peggy Kirk Bell, who teaches some 800 women a year to play golf at Pine Needles Golf Course in Southern Pines, N.C., and who played on the 1950 Curtis Cup team, remembers her non-playing captain, Glenna Collett, as a woman of few words. She also remembers Glenna's response when her patience was tested. During the traditional lunch before the first match of the Curtis Cup, the captain of the British team, Diana Critchley, addressed the group.

"Now Diana had beaten Glenna in the British Open in 1930," Peggy Bell says. "She hadn't beaten her before, nor did she after that. She had a lucky day. Diana said from the podium, 'I hope my team can do to your team what I did to your captain a few years ago.' I looked at Glenna, and she was livid. She hated making speeches, but she got up. She said, 'I just hope the best team wins—this time.'"

For Peggy Bell, making the Curtis Cup team was a dream come true. Playing for Collett made the reality doubly intense because Collett had been Bell's heroine when Peggy was a teenager. "She had a fast swing," Bell recalls. "Her left heel would come up for just a moment at the end of her back swing and she'd put it down fast and firmly as she swung. Up! Down! She played fast. She went to the ball, put her club down, and hit it. No practice swings. She had it figured out. She thought you should play eighteen holes in two-and-a-half hours. That intimidated a lot of people."

The night before her Curtis Cup match, Bell got cold feet. Overcome with the idea of playing for her country, Bell went to Glenna Collett's room and beseeched her coach, "'Please don't play me. I couldn't stand it if I lost.' Glenna looked at me and said, 'I'm the captain, and you're playing.' "

The next day, all even with her opponent, Jean Bisgood, after sixteen holes, Peggy Bell spotted her coach walking in the rough, following the match. Collett motioned Bell over. "She handed me a four-leaf clover," Bell says. "She had a knack for finding them. And she looked me in the eye and said, 'Go get her.'" Bell won the match on the eighteenth hole with a stymie, a now-extinct rule that created an impasse for the player whose ball was farthest from the cup, when the opponent's ball was blocking the path more than six inches from the cup.

Glenna Collett was that magic combination of star player and gracious ambassador. She was a publicist's dream at a time when women were beginning to reach out, enter politics, swim the English Channel, fly across the Atlantic. She maintained that two of the rights women had won by 1925 were exercising their suffrage and participating in sports. And Collett had an elegant way of expressing herself that made any woman with the least interest in golf practically drool with anticipation as she was moved to run—not walk—to the nearest golf course. "The long undulation of fairway," Collett wrote in her autobiography, "like a flowing river caressed by sun and wind, the white and regular splashes of bunkers, the sparkling emerald of the

From left: Gene Sarazen, Joyce Wethered, Glenna Collett Vare, and Johnny Dawson played an exhibition match in 1935 to honor Miss Wethered's American professional debut.

putting greens, with red flags fluttering astern over cups, unrolled for me much like a magic carpet over which I blithely walked to the heights."

Now that she had them at the golf course, Collett further increased women's enthusiasm by putting winning in perspective. "There is an ideal," Collett wrote, "beyond the goal of mere winning: a high appraisal of one's self. Even in sport there are people who put a valuation on themselves that they are not willing to mark down, no matter what happens . . . they try to be good losers, and when their valuation is challenged, they lose . . . without a gesture."

Shamelessly shilling the sport at which she excelled and deeply loved, Collett went on to extol the virtues of golf regarding health, fitness, weight control . . . and romance. "Unhappy love affairs," she wrote, "will not concern a girl made strong in the sun. The girl golfer would, instead of fretting and brooding, pick up her golf clubs and concentrate on making the next hole rather than stay in bed tortured by introspection." If more women played golf, Collett maintained, "the beauty parlors would not be so full of middle-aged women seeking a synthetic youth."

She even tendered advice to parents about getting their daughters started in the sport that is still valid seventy-five years later: get them good clubs; give them lessons from a tried professional; take them to watch famous players in a tournament.

Collett told it like it was. Perhaps the most admirable thing about Glenna Collett is that she was a woman of her time, and proud of it. In response to writer William Richardson's question about how the best women golfers would do against the best men golfers, head-to-head, Collett's answer was short and to the point. Citing the inequality of men's and women's forearms and wrists, she told Richardson, "women lack the strength to play golf as well as men."

Reflecting her era, she said that strength on the links is an asset, but not a requirement. "A woman needs more strokes because she is a woman," Collett wrote, reasoning that first of all, a woman cares as much about her appearance as she does her score. Collett was, of course, dealing with the formal dress code of the 1920s. She had written about how Cecil Leitch had her skirts made just wide enough to accommodate her widest stance. Many women compromised their stance in the interest of avoiding the dowdiness of such a fashion-contrary garment. As Collett said, "There is a limit even in the pursuit of par."

Vanity was only part of it. While the wide-hemmed skirt was fine for driving, on the more closed stance shots (approaches, putting), the folds of such a large skirt could be whipped by the wind, creating unsteadiness, temporary blind spots, and interference with the club. Of course if it rains, inappropriate clothing could cause a disaster, as it did for one of Collett's opponents, Canadian champion Ada Mackenzie, during a match in the early 1920s. "Miss Mackenzie was wearing a knitted suit which reached just below her knees. As the rain fell harder, the soaked skirt grew longer, and finally reached to her shoe tops. It is no simple matter to drive with a soaked skirt clinging to your legs."

Last of all Collett spoke of form. She said men don't care if they look awkward off the tee. A long ball down the middle is worth any awkward moment they might suffer. But a woman might shorten her swing if she thinks that a graceful appearance might be compromised by her efforts to really give one a ride. "She has a duty more important than golf—the age-old feminine duty never to look ridiculous if she can help it," said Collett.

Collett worked diligently at being a great golfer but not at the expense of her femininity, as perceived in the 1920s in the United States. When she was asked to consider the Olympian heights of golf, she balked, saying she knew of no woman who ever gave it a thought. "[We might] cut off our hair to keep the flying ringlets from bothering while we putt; train our muscles to obey the brain's behest. But to make our bodies hard as nails by muscular training, or to get our heads to the state of baldness to acquire greatness in golf is far beyond our desires. When women think about the winning of everything in golf it will be time to worry."

By no means does Collett wring her hands over the feminine handicaps she enumerates. The "burden" of womanhood, for Glenna Collett, was a torch she carried with obvious ease and considerable pride. Humorist James Thurber would later summarize the complex coexistence of the sexes as "the war between men and women." In that contest, Glenna Collett loved the side she was on.

GROWING UP GOLFING

"The kids used to complain when the wind was blowing. I used to tell them never let the wind know. It's the same for everyone."

ROSANN CLARK ELDRIDGE

ROSANN CLARK ELDRIDGE WON the Tampa Bay Women's Championship four years in a row, from 1936 to 1939. That was a major accomplishment in the sunshine state of Florida, where the availability of golf year-round guaranteed its early popularity. But what's even more remarkable is the diminutive Miss Clark (5'2", 116 pounds), a working-class girl competing against a field of society ladies who spent their copious leisure time on the links. Today, Rosann Clark Eldridge is eighty-two years old. Her idea of a good day is hitting 300 balls at the driving range.

Rosann Clark (at right) loved sports as a child. With her seven brothers and sisters she played basketball, softball, and remembers walking four miles a day, barefoot. She grew up across the street from a golf course, became a caddy as soon as she could lift a bag, and quickly got a club of her own. "I had a cut-down five-iron," she recalls, "and I could do anything with it—drive, chip, or putt." When she wasn't caddying, she worked in the pro shop assembling clubs and restoring old balls. "The balls in those days had soft covers that cut easily. We'd peel the covers off the cut balls and unwind the elastic. The center had paint in it. We used that paint to dress up the old balls without cuts and sell 'em for five or ten cents, depending on how good they looked. Those were depression days." She assembled her own first set of clubs.

Her brothers were also good young golfers. Robert won the men's Tampa Bay City Championship one of the years Rosann won the women's. He taught Rosann to get out of bunkers, something he was particularly good at. "We went out on the course, and he dropped two balls into a sand trap," she recalls. "Then he chipped both of them into the cup. He said to me, 'That's how you do it,' and walked off."

In 1936, Rosann was the long drive winner at the Tampa Bay tournament with a drive of 201 yards. "The women played from the same tees as the men," she recalls. "And on the tee there was a box of builders' sand. You scooped up some and made a little mound to set your ball on, because the golf tee hadn't come along yet."

Rosann wasn't tempted to turn professional. Her heroes were the great amateurs. But having a covey of her own children got her started teaching. "Golf changes kids' lives because of what they learn about manners and etiquette. On a golf course you're expected to rake sand traps, pick up divots, clean up your mess."

In addition to her four Tampa Bay titles, Rosann Clark Eldridge has won her local Ft. Meyers Club Championship seven times. In 1959, she won it in February. She delivered a daughter one month later.

HYANNIS PORT, MASSACHUSETTS Located on a salty Cape Cod rise of fertile land that overlooks Squaw Island and Nantucket Sound, the Hyannis Port Club's original six-hole course was laid out in 1897. Some of the tees and putting greens were on private land. Several women are listed among the first stockholders at the club's incorporation in 1909. The status of women players is reflected in one handsome sterling silver trophy for a women's tournament that is dated 1902.

HYANNIS PORT

3 THE PROMOTERS

THE POPULARIZATION OF ANY MOVEMENT DEPENDS to a large extent on style and timing. Women's golf has been fortunate in both regards. Glenna Collett was the ideal figurehead for her era. Soft-spoken, conservative, and unfailingly high-minded, Collett's style, her regal presence at the top of her sport sent a message to women that taking up golf would not compromise their dignity, detract from their femininity, nor tarnish their social standing.

Patty Berg and Babe Didrickson Zaharias, the two most prominent golfers to follow in Collett's footsteps, were also powerful stylists. But unlike Collett, both of them had rough edges. They were strong, flamboyant women who loved a challenge as much as a spicy joke. Each cultivated an intimidating presence. And unlike Collett, the two didn't put much stock in society's conventions. Neither shied from the limelight. Together, Berg and Zaharias would define the structure of women's professional golf. But like their predecessor, they were just right for their time. In the 1930s, with the ominous rumblings emanating from Europe that would erupt into World War II, the lighthearted aggressiveness displayed by Berg and Zaharias as they took the woman's golf world by storm suggested a formula for survival in the difficult years to come.

Glenna Collett had to be lured away from the baseball diamond to play golf. With Patty Berg, it was football. A stocky youngster who also liked speed skating, Patty quarterbacked a neighborhood team started by Bud Wilkinson, the man who would go on to engineer the Oklahoma Sooners football dynasty of the 1950s. Like the Colletts, the Bergs were well-off. Patty's father was a grain merchant. He was also a golfer with a ten handicap, a member of the well-

Patty Berg (left) and Babe Zaharias after finishing their rounds at the Women's Western Open in Park Ridge, Ill., in 1944.

known Interlachen Club in Minneapolis. When he gave his son a membership to the club, his daughter bristled and demanded one as well. So he signed her up for lessons, and at fifteen she qualified for the 1933 Minneapolis City Championship with a score of 122. She lost in the first round and made a decision to give the game her full attention for a year. In *The Illustrated History of Women's Golf*, Rhonda Glenn quotes Patty Berg as she recalled that moment in her life: "That was the turning point in my whole career, because if I hadn't improved in 365 days, I don't think I would be in golf today." The next year, sixteen-year-old Berg won the Minneapolis City Championship.

Just a year later, she entered the Women's National Amateur Championship, mainly because it was being held at Interlachen. Berg played brilliantly, and to everyone's amazement, she made the finals. She lost to the formidable Glenna Collett after battling back on the second nine to a near victory.

In 1936, *Time* magazine called Patty Berg "the most promising golfer since the appearance of Glenna herself." That year, the eighteen-year-old Berg took the qualifying medal of the Women's South Atlantic Championships with a score of 73 before losing in the final. A week later she beat Collett in the second round of another tournament before losing in the final. Berg would go on to win twenty-eight amateur titles in the course of the next seven years, including three Titleholders (the ladies' equivalent of the Masters, discontinued in 1972), and the U.S. Women's Amateur (1938). She was on two Curtis Cup teams and received the first of her three Associated Press Athlete of the Year awards in 1938. She amassed sixty career victories and won fifteen major tournaments.

The small but dedicated band that followed women's amateur golf in the late 1930s knew that Patty Berg had brought something special to the game. Berg turned professional in 1940 and was unexpectedly sidelined for eighteen months after breaking her knee in a car crash in 1941. She was off the course for another three years (1942–1945) while she served in the Marines as a lieutenant during World War II. Still, the irrepressible Berg's full-tilt approach to the game had a profound influence on women's golf. Her dedicated effort made that

Patty Berg at eighteen, playing at the Palm Beach Country Club's city championship in 1937. She placed eighth in the qualifying round.

happen because in the pre-television and videotape days, the personal appearance was the only effective way to spread the word. Her father had drummed one notion into her head: give back. And that became her gospel. As Patty Berg had applied herself to excel at golf, she would also teach, encourage, and motivate with the same passion. Rhonda Glenn recalled the fire of Patty's oft-repeated speech about what it takes to be a champion: "she hit you with it, shouting at you about the will to win, inspiration, never giving up, desire, self-control, determination, heart, courage, striving for perfection, faith, aiming at the top . . . she was Winston Churchill and FDR rolled into one."

When Patty was playing amateur golf tournaments, her father would schedule charity appearances for her on weekends, which escalated into a full schedule of exhibitions on the road with other prominent amateurs. The process of inventing interesting formats for these demonstrations made Patty Berg aware of her natural affinity for the stage. Those early road trips were the catalyst for the traveling golf and comedy shows that Patty Berg made famous. With an eye to the future, she began polishing her skills by watching Helen Hicks, a Women's Amateur Champion whom the Wilson Sporting Goods Company had hired in 1935 to promote their equipment line by giving demonstrations. Just five years later, Patty Berg turned pro by signing with Wilson, and the agreement would prove to be a lifelong relationship. Players like to joke that Patty Berg's major commitments are to God and Wilson Sporting Goods, and not necessarily in that order.

Wilson's CEO in the 1930s was an innovator named L. B. Icely, who is credited with first identifying the now-common notion that accomplished athletes could be a company's best promoters. The clinics Icely underwrote for ladies' golf were a boon for Wilson's salesmen and did wonders to promote golf for women all over the country.

Joe Phillips saw what the clinics did for the business of selling golf

In 1943, Berg is sworn into the Marine Corps. In 1941, Berg and Opal Hill (dark sweater) showed Navy cadets in San Diego how to get a grip.

equipment. Phillips joined Wilson in 1948, eventually becoming vice president for promotion. His responsibilities included promoting the LPGA and PGA tours, and 1,100 club professionals. Phillips retired in 1989, but remains a consultant for Wilson.

After arranging for three or four women professionals to make an appearance at a particular club, Phillips would extend invitations to all clubs in the area. It was free. Two or three hundred people would usually attend. Wilson sold a lot of golf clubs because of those clinics.

"We used to work the players hard. We'd often do two clinics per day. One in the morning, followed by lunch, where the 'students' could talk to the players. Then we'd go off to another club and do a second clinic in the after-noon, followed by dinner. In the evening I'd set up an interview for the players at the local TV station."

Nobody could run a clinic quite like Patty Berg. She gave more than 2,000 of them. A videotape of a Berg golf clinic was shot in 1995 by Chicago independent television producer, Curt Petersen. Patty's energy that day belied her seventy-five years. The club professional gave her a short introduction: "And now, the Patty Berg Golf Show. Please welcome Miss Golf USA, Patty Berg." Patty, in matching blue slacks and top, wearing a white Wilson cap with "Patty" embroidered on one side, hustled on stage. The "stage" was a plot of golf grass overlooking a pond that had been defined with several dozen American flags on sticks. Patty Berg was a short, sturdy woman at that moment in her life, with trimmed, curly blond hair. She walked at attention with little snappy steps, her arms pumping as if she were marching. "They call me Patrick Henry Dynamite Berg," she said, and like any good talk show host, she smartly threw the praise back to the professional who had introduced her as she kept marching toward the camera, then back-stepping away, an old vaudeville move that involved a series of expansive gestures culminating in a low bow.

She told her audience of mostly women and youngsters that her show would be in three acts: "Act one, scene one, the irons. Act two, scene two, sisters. Act three, scene three, the woods. Stay for all three acts. Anyone who leaves is a

Patty Berg on stage during one of her famous golf clinics in the late 1970s. Berg retired from com-petition in 1980 but has never left golf.

The clinics also helped the early professionals make ends meet at a time when a tournament win might be worth $100. Initially, the players got expense money for clinics, which often got them to tournament sites. Only later were they paid to do the clinics as well.

Estimates indicate that Patty Berg traveled an average of 60,000 miles a year doing classes, clinics, and exhibitions until she was forced to slow her pace in 1991. She has probably had more direct effect on the growth and development of the women's game than any golfer in history. At the turn of the twenty-first century, Patty Berg was in her eighties, living in Florida. There's hardly a junior or benefit tournament in the state over the past sixty years that she hasn't graced with her presence.

Berg's friend, rival, and partner in professionalism was the late Mildred "Babe" Didrikson Zaharias, golf's first female "rock star." Only if Michael Jordan were to become a professional golfer and began winning with frequency would there be a comparison to the fanfare that accompanied Babe Didrikson's entry into the sport. In the early 1950s, woman's golf was still in its adolescence, and the media was a far cry from the all-pervasive giant of today. But Babe's impact on the sport, for its time, was immense.

Generally acknowledged as the greatest female athlete of the century—number ten on ESPN's 1999 series, "The Fifty Greatest Athletes"—Babe had the boastful exuberance that often accompanies legendary accomplishment. She took up golf after winning two gold medals (eighty-meter hurdles and javelin) at the 1932 Olympics. She won a third gold in the high jump but was disqualified for rolling over the bar at a world record height, face up, a technique that is both legal and preferred today. She was the complete athlete. There was nothing requiring hand-to-eye coordination, strength, agility, endurance, stamina, and confidence that Babe couldn't do, including dancing. There were even more arrows in her quiver. She played a mean harmonica, cooked, sewed, typed like a stenographer, and had a gift for gab that matched her willingness to lock horns with just about anyone. Her often ribald sense of humor was well known. Her

Babe Zaharias in her prime in 1946, winning the All-American women's title at Tam O'Shanter with a medal round of 70, and an average of 77.

brashness was feared and sometimes disparaged. Competition was her lifeblood.

Didrikson had played golf a few times in her teens. Gerald Astor wrote in *The PGA World Golf Hall of Fame Book* that it was sportswriter Grantland Rice who got Babe to play golf. In the press box during the last day of the 1932 Olympics, Rice mentioned he couldn't think of a sport that the Babe couldn't master. Someone suggested golf as one that would give her trouble. Rice, who was a close friend of Babe's, sent word to her on the field, and soon she appeared in the press box. A game was set for the following day.

Babe held the club like a baseball bat and swung for the rafters. But she drove the ball 250 yards off the tee. She swung so hard she'd fall back after every tee shot, a quirk of her game that never left her. Her score was 95, not bad for

Left to right: Babe hitting balls at Yankee Stadium in 1948; as a member of the professional Brooklyn Yankees in 1933; running track at the 1932 Olympics.

her first serious round. Hitting the ball was simple for an athlete of Babe's abilities. All it required was muscle coordination and timing. But the difference between playing golf and playing *championship* golf is huge. The late Fred Corcoran, PGA tournament director in the 1930s and 1940s, would become Babe's agent in 1948. In his book, *Unplayable Lies*, Corcoran wrote that golf was one game Babe couldn't bully into submission. "She found par a tireless and unyielding opponent. Golf offered a fresh challenge every time she picked up a club."

Having decided she liked golf, Babe approached it as she did everything else—with total immersion. She took lessons and began arduous practice sessions that lasted eight to ten hours a day. She'd hit as many as 1,500 balls a session, causing her hands to blister and bleed.

Babe winning gold medals and setting Olympic (javelin) and world (80-meter hurdles) records at the 1932 Olympic Games in Los Angeles.

By 1934, Didrikson was playing the amateur circuit. She ran into trouble at the Texas State Championship in 1935. Gerald Astor wrote: "Peggy Chandler, a member of the Texas Woman's Golf Association sniffed: 'We don't need any truck driver's daughters in this tournament.'" Didrikson's father was, in fact, a carpenter. Mrs. Chandler was just expressing, however regrettably, the resentment many women *and* men felt about Babe. After all, she was an anomaly, a female athlete several cuts above any that had ever existed. Her abilities made her suspect. Even women athletes didn't come in such muscular packages. Her face was a little too lean, her smile a little too crooked. And she was too sassy, too full of herself. She was, to a society matron of Mrs. Chandler's ilk, common. Perhaps if Babe hadn't been such a good golfer there wouldn't have been an issue. But Mrs. Chandler's designs on winning the tournament herself were obviously compromised by Babe's presence.

And as luck would have it, Babe would meet the snobbish Mrs. Chandler in the thirty-six-hole final. After a shaky start, Babe drew even and no doubt disrupted Mrs. Chandler's concentration on the thirty-fourth hole by sinking an impossible sand wedge out of a mud puddle for an eagle. The two halved the thirty-fifth, and Babe won it on the final hole. Her win was popular in the press, but not with the authorities, who used her professional status, announced by the Amateur Athletic Union, to bar her from further amateur golf tournaments.

So Babe turned pro and began playing exhibitions with the best men, players like Gene Sarazen and Sam Snead. She was the first female pro to have a trainer, and she commanded the same $1,000 appearance fees as Byron Nelson and Ben Hogan. And Babe began banging the drum for the professional cause, recruiting hard among the amateur ranks. When amateurs pointed out there were no professional tournaments for women, she told them no worries, there will *be* tournaments.

Babe raised a few more eyebrows by marrying professional wrestler George Zaharias, a bear of a man whose ring moniker was "The Crying Greek from Cripple Creek." Zaharias's act was to weep during his matches. Babe asked George to quit wrestling, which he did. He became a promoter, and at one time owned a piece of the Los Angeles Rams. The press loved this match made in media heaven. The Babe story grew livelier and more entertaining.

Peggy Kirk Bell spent a lot of time with Babe Zaharias. As an aspiring amateur, Peggy met Babe at the Western Amateur Tournament in Chicago in the mid-1940s. "She was on the range, hitting practice balls. I moved in for a closer look. She was hitting them a mile. I noticed she had a glove, so I went out and got one. Later I was passing through the locker room, and there was Babe, sitting alone at a table, shuffling cards. She said 'Hey kid, want to play some gin? I'll teach you.' Me? I couldn't believe it. So I sat down. It was that Hollywood game

Mr. and Mrs. George Zaharias share a hot dog while awaiting official news of Babe's victory in the 1944 Women's Western Open in Illinois.

with three rows, ten cards in a row. We played for awhile. Then Babe said, 'Okay kid, you owe me $12.30.' That was big money. I didn't know we were playing for money. But I paid her. She asked me if I wanted a chance to get even. I wasn't that dumb. I got outta there." But a friendship was born.

"She called me not long after that. 'Peggy? It's the Babe.' She asked me if I was planning to be in Florida that winter. She needed a partner for the Hollywood Women's International Four-Ball Tournament. She said, 'You may as well play with me and win one.' She'd won the first seven tournaments she played that year, 1947. I agreed, but I was nervous. I told her if we lost, it would be my fault. She told me not to worry. She said, 'I can beat any two of them without you. I'll let you know if I need you.'" They won.

"Babe had a lot of presence," Peggy Bell says. "She was smart, entertaining, she had it all figured out. We were at dinner one night in a fancy restaurant, my dad, George, Babe, and me. A distinguished-looking man approached the table to speak with Babe. He excused himself and said to Babe that he and his friends had recognized her and were discussing how far she had thrown the javelin. Could she help them out? 'Further than anyone else in the world,' she told him, and laughed. About ten minutes later, she got up, pulled her chair over to the man's table, and said, 'Okay, let's talk about me.'"

The two women had dinner one night before they had to play a finals match against each other the next day. Peggy Bell admits she was nervous, a little on edge about it. "During dinner, Babe noticed my mood. 'You don't think you have a chance of beating me, do you?' she asked. She was that way. People either loved her or hated her. She'd be on the first tee, and as she walked to place her ball she'd say, 'Come on, I'll show you how to play.' Once I saw her hit an iron out of the rough over an impossibly high tree to within a few feet of the pin. It was a great shot. She turned to us with a smile and said, 'Don't you wish you could do that?' It wasn't mean. It was just Babe.

"She was a long hitter. She used the big muscles in her back to get the ball off the tee. She was playing with Sam Snead one time, and hit a very long

Peggy Kirk mops the brow of Babe Zaharias after Babe had beaten her friend Kirk in the opening round of the 1951 Women's Western Open.

drive. She turned to Sam and said, 'See if you can catch that one.' Snead came up a foot short. He wanted to know where she'd gotten her ball."

Babe Zaharias used everything in her arsenal to promote herself, and why not? She was a professional. She'd become a media darling during the Olympics, learning what a powerful ally the press could be. Having a professional wrestler as a husband no doubt helped. No one understands the value of illusion better than a professional wrestler. But more than anything, Babe was a natural at working the press. She always had a story for them, and the press loved her, helped her become the primary drawing card for women's professional golf. She loved the attention, and she had a devilish streak that leapt to the forefront when the microphones and notebooks came out. She once told the press she was planning to play in the men's U.S. Open. It was a total fabrication, but it made a great story. And it generated anxiety for a lot of male players. Tournament authorities quickly drafted a rule prohibiting women from playing in the U.S. Open.

Fred Corcoran tells the story about one night in Yankee Stadium when Babe stood on the diamond and hit golf balls out of sight. Then she grabbed a glove and took infield practice. She ripped her skirt up the front so it wouldn't get in the way and handled herself like a big leaguer, scooping up ground balls and firing them to first. The crowd was amazed, surely filled with mixed emotions. For the men in the stands who played amateur ball, their admiration had to be tempered by the threat implied by a woman showing such competence as an infielder. And those women who weren't looking down their nose at such an undignified display had to be experiencing a heady vision of what was possible. That was the effect Babe had on people.

"We were in Denver one time getting ready for a tournament," Peggy Bell recalls. "Babe and I played a practice round together. Afterwards, the press gathered around her. 'What did you shoot,' they wanted to know. Babe told them she had a 71. They all rushed off to write their stories, and I said to Babe, 'Wait a minute, you had a 77.' And she said, 'Well, I should have had a 71. Besides, I tell them what they want to hear.' And there it was in the next day's paper, 'Babe warms up with a 71.' That shook up the competition."

Peggy Bell says she always chuckles when she hears the story that Arnold Palmer was the first golfer ever to receive a Rolex watch. She knows that the first golfer ever to get a Rolex was a woman. "Babe and I were in New York. She was doing the "Ed Sullivan Show." Walking down Fifth Avenue we looked into a shop window, and there on display were the first Rolex watches for women. Well, Babe got all excited, said she had to have one. So we caught a cab and went up to Rolex headquarters. Babe walked in and asked to speak with the president. They asked if she had an appointment. She said no, just tell him Babe Didrikson Zaharias is here. Well, in about ten seconds the president came out, totally delighted, and off we went to lunch at Toots Shor's. Babe charmed him to death, and told him she had to have one of the new ladies' Rolexes. He said of course, no problem. Then she looked at him and said, 'George needs one, too.'"

Many have said that Patty Berg suffered under the celebrity power of Zaharias and the way the Babe used the media to exploit herself. The press has often commented on Berg's "second fiddle" role to Babe, and other players have deplored the shadow cast upon Berg's skill by the Babe's bright star. But no such complaints have ever been voiced by the gracious Miss Berg. Their head-to-head record speaks for itself. In their many meetings, Berg only lost once to the Babe. When pressed for this fact, Berg gives it the back of her hand. "I hit her on bad days," she says. And Berg continues to speak of her old rival with heartfelt esteem and admiration. In an interview a few years ago, Berg expressed sadness that Babe passed on before she saw the results of her efforts to open doors for women and sports. "There is no question she opened those doors," Berg said. "She was really something. She did so much for the game."

It was the combination of Berg and Zaharias that gave women's golf a powerful identity through the war years and set the stage for the growth it would enjoy in the 1950s. Neither golfer knew it, but the two were a team. With Babe making the headlines and Patty bringing the game to the masses with her clinics, women's golf was in good hands.

THE RIGHT CLUB

"The women's marketplace was vacant. There were many products, but none spoke to women's needs. Women don't want a version of a man's club."

CINDY DAVIS

OF ALL THE CONSTRAINTS ON women golfers, from gender discrimination to outrageous fashion getups, none has endured quite as long as the scarcity of proper equipment. It has been proven that any golfer's game will be advanced by using clubs that are compatible with height, weight, arm length, and swing speed. Because most women don't have the muscle mass of a man, using proper equipment is especially apropos for women golfers. And yet until recently little attention had been paid to customizing clubs for women. Time after time one hears stories about young women golfers getting started with a set of "cut down" men's clubs.

In the days of clubs with hickory shafts, when woods were wood, all golfers did the best they could with what was available. It is amazing how well the best women of the day played with equipment so inadequate by today's standards. We can only imagine what early women champions would have done with a bag full of perimeter-weighted irons and steel or titanium woods. Naturally they would be hitting the latest space-age dyno-wound double-covered balls made of materials like Ionomer, gel, polybutadilene, thermoelastomer Surlyn, or maybe Neodymium, and imprinted with more than 300 dimples whose shape is computer modeled and tested in wind tunnels. There are several balls designed for women currently on the market. They tend to be softer, lower compression balls that respond better to a slower swing speed.

There have been clubs marketed for ladies since the 1920s, but not much engineering has gone into them. They weren't all that different from men's clubs. It's only in the last few years that women's golf equipment has gotten comprehensive attention. The design, manufacture, and marketing of women's golf clubs are currently undergoing what Cindy Davis calls "a shift in paradigm in the culture of the industry." Davis is former CEO of Arnold Palmer Golf and Nancy Lopez Golf. She says that when she joined Nancy Lopez in 1997, research indicated that women felt both overwhelmed and intimidated when it came to purchasing golf clubs. "Within the retail shops and even the pro shops, there wasn't much real estate devoted to women's golf," Davis says.

Not only did Davis and Lopez innovate the fitting of clubs by making choices of grip size, shaft length, and flexibility available off the pro-shop rack, they began paying attention to what made women comfortable at the point of purchase. "I have to admit," Davis says, "we borrowed a few ideas from Saturn. They have done a great job selling cars to women. We applied some of the same concepts. We let women know we have their interests and needs at heart. It's all about delivering a quality product that works and inspires confidence."

SANTA CRUZ, CALIFORNIA In 1928, from horseback on the rolling land above Santa Cruz, Marion Hollins first envisioned a planned community of houses surrounding a multi-sports facility. Alister MacKenzie designed the golf course, but this time Hollins was so involved that MacKenzie referred to her as his "associate." Among the early visitors to Pasatiempo were Glenna Collett, Bobby Jones, Joyce Wethered, and a young woman named Babe Didrickson, who was just learning to play golf.

of the Weathervane Tournament. Testament to Corcoran's famed powers of persuasion, Mrs. Lengfeld did the job without compensation. Not that Mrs. Lengfeld needed the money. Heiress to a double family fortune, it was golf's good luck that this tomboy discovered the game when she was just eight years old. At a hotel in Pasadena, Calif., where her family wintered and where she first learned to play golf, a person she described as "a nice little man in a red vest" often played with her because she was about his size (4' 8"). The man was Andrew Carnegie.

Lengfeld became a lifetime devotee of the game. She competed with success as an amateur, and her pioneering efforts on the administrative end did wonders to promote golf for women. In 1926 she won the San Francisco Women's Championship. In 1927 she won the Championship of the Women's Golf Association of Northern California at Lakeside, an organization she helped found. While president of the WGANC, Lengfeld started the California Women's Golf Circuit, a tour that made it possible for every woman golfer to play all others. Both Babe Zaharias and Patty Berg played on that circuit. Lengfeld also started the Pacific Women's Golf Association to represent women who were not members of country clubs.

As with her other wide-ranging charitable work, promoting golf was a philanthropic venture for Helen Lengfeld. She personally covered the expenses of many tournaments she sponsored, counting any attendance money as profits. As Elinor Nicholson suggested in her book, *Golf, A Women's History*, "[Lengfeld's approach] may be one way of distinguishing a philanthropist from a charitable fund-raiser."

Corcoran selected wisely. In 1951, Helen Lengfeld arranged for the first Weathervane Tournament to start at famed Pebble Beach. Her guiding hand was evident as the tour made its way across the country from California to Dallas, Indianapolis, and finally White Plains, N.Y. Those who played were a who's who of women golfers with names that are still familiar today: Patty Berg, Babe Zaharias, Betty Jameson, Alice and Marlene Bauer, Helen Dettweiler, Betsy Rawls, Betty Bush, Betty McKinnon, Shirley Spork, Peggy Kirk, Marilynn Smith, and Louise Suggs.

A smiling Betsy Rawls points to her winning margin at the 1951 Women's Open as Patty Berg, Louise Suggs, and Babe Zaharias feign dismay.

Louise Suggs turned pro in 1948, a particularly good year for her. Suggs had burst onto the amateur scene when she was seventeen, winning her first important tournaments during the war years. Her father, John Suggs, a former baseball player, owned a public golf course he built in Lithia Springs, near Atlanta, Ga. He was the resident pro there. When she was thirteen, Louise was spotted hitting balls on the range by the then Georgia State women's champion, Martha Daniel. Miss Daniel sought out John Suggs and talked him into letting his daughter play in the state championship. She lost in the first round. The following year she was runner-up. The next year Louise Suggs won the tournament. "The lady I beat in the semi-finals had kids older than me," Suggs recalls. "She resented it."

In 1948, after winning the Women's British Open, the Women's U.S. Amateur Championship (the only player ever to win those tournaments in the same year), and being named to the U.S. Curtis Cup team, Suggs had become one of the hottest golfers in the country. When Suggs returned from Europe, she recalls that representatives from Wilson, MacGregor, and Spalding were on hand to meet the boat. She and her father decided upon MacGregor, where they figured Louise would become the first and therefore senior female member of the staff. "But my dad held back. He said let's think about this. He was a good agent. We went out to Cincinnati to MacGregor's headquarters to meet the president, Henry Cowen. Dad told Mr. Cowen I should get a $5,000 bonus up front. Cowen agreed. That was huge! Seven years before I had been working as a file clerk for $25 a week. Now I had a signing bonus. It might have been the first one ever."

Henry Cowen, a vigorous ninety-one years old in 1999, says that Louise Suggs was not his first female staffer. Cowen says that MacGregor had Babe Zaharias under contract for a year. Then she left MacGregor and went to Wilson. But in 1948, when Suggs showed up, the decks were cleared. "We needed women staffers," Cowen says. "From a marketing standpoint, we saw women's golf as a growing thing. The press took hold of it, and the market began to click. Those early tournaments got things going. Equipment sales went up as the sport caught fire in America. When Fred Corcoran came into the LPGA, he was a major force,

The field for a Red Cross benefit tournament at Pinehurst, N.C., in 1951 was (seated from left): Shirley Speck, Betty Bush, Betty MacKinnon, and Peggy Kirk. Standing (from left): Marlene Bauer, Alice Bauer, runner-up Babe Zaharias, and winner Patty Berg.

a promoter from the word go. He had a way with the press, always had a story for them. He gave us tips on which good amateurs were thinking of turning pro."

The big three—MacGregor, Spalding, and Wilson—worked their staffers hard. Booking dates through country club pros and stores where their sponsor's products were sold, the women gave exhibitions all over the country. Peggy Bell remembers hitting balls in Sears Roebuck stores to promote her signature Spalding clubs. The women played against local pros and the best women amateurs, raising money for charity along the way. And Fred Corcoran kept his ear to the ground, feeding the sport's growth by dropping ideas in the right places at the right time, orchestrating deals, promoting his female charges full time.

"Corcoran let me know," Henry Cowen says, "about a women's sportswear manufacturer that was looking for a golfer who would put her name on a line of sportswear. I recall it was the David H. Smith Company of Lynn, Mass. We contacted them, suggested Louise Suggs, and they took her. With Suggs' name on their line, David H. Smith did something they'd been trying to do for many years. They got their clothing into Saks Fifth Avenue. It was Suggs' name that did it. So in addition to her other duties, Louise had a schedule of personal appearances in Saks."

At seventy-six, Louise Suggs is a robust woman with a trim cap of gray hair. She still plays golf and teaches at the Cloisters, on Sea Island, Ga. Her calm blue eyes set against her permanent golfer's tan are quietly challenging. Her reputation as a stoic, no-nonsense person is well-deserved. As a player, she let her game do the talking, and it spoke with eloquence. She still has a strong, fluid swing, and in her prime she had a way of stalking a golf course that was compelling. Nowadays she's a bit more forthcoming. When asked about Fred Corcoran, she smiled. "I once asked him if he would be my agent. He said no. I asked him why. 'Because you're too goddamned honest,' he said. And he was serious. He ran his business out of his hip pocket. It was messy. But he did the job, put tournaments together. He was a promoter."

Louise Suggs was short-fused when it came to the antics of Babe Didrickson. "Either it went her way, or she was difficult," Suggs says. "People had to sit on her as much as possible. When George Zaharias came on the scene, it got worse. Babe would just walk on into the men's locker room if she pleased. We had a rule in the LPGA that there would be no appearance fees. But Babe had her own deals. The rest of us couldn't do anything about it. We were starved for tournaments."

To improve that situation, Suggs and her father used to co-host an annual tournament at a Trent Jones–designed course called Sunset Hills in Carrollton, Ga. John Suggs also built that course. The social side of women's tournaments was important from the start, so the Suggs family always planned a big dinner, followed by dancing at Sunset Hills.

The early tournaments were do-it-yourself affairs. The women carpooled and lived out of their trunks. They changed in their cars. One of the players could type, so she became the secretary. All of them pitched in to set pins, mark the courses, set up the tees, and make rules decisions. Often the courses were so bad that farm implements had to be used to define the fairways. It was a tough day-to-day grind.

The galleries were often big, out of curiosity if nothing more, and the spectators walked along with the players. "You'd hit," Louise Suggs says, "and the gallery would close in and you wouldn't even see the ball land. Once I was playing an exhibition in Duneeden, Fla. The hole was a dogleg right. And there was the gallery, about 120 yards away, and right *in* the way of where I wanted to hit. So I waved them back. Some of them moved, so I hit my drive. I heard this bad sound, and a man in the gallery dropped to the ground like he'd been shot. The ball hit him right in the chest. I got all of it, and it got all of him. He was white as a sheet. Luckily, the ball had hit the metal glasses case in his breast pocket. Otherwise he might have been dead."

Suggs was the first woman to regularly take on the best men and beat them. One of the first head-to-head competitions between men and women was in Palm Beach, where an entrepreneur named Mike Phipps built a par-three course in the mid-1950s. It was a beautiful, difficult course bracketed by Lake Worth on one side and the Atlantic Ocean on the other. One hole measured 225 yards. Part of the course dedication was a fifty-four-hole tournament involving a dozen each of the best men and women professionals and amateurs—forty-eight players in all. Suggs won the tournament with a score of four under par. Among the men she beat were Frank Stranahan, Cary Middlecoff, and Sam Snead.

"Snead was so mad he couldn't see straight," Louise says. In the clubhouse afterwards he was really going after me, laying it on. So I said to him, 'Sam, what are you so mad about . . . you didn't even finish second.' Well, he tore out of there. You could hear his tires laying rubber as he pulled out of the parking lot."

Louise Suggs also remembers that the prize money for the tournament was, as usual, about 50 percent more for the men than the women. But when Suggs won overall, the check Mike Phipps sent her was the same as if a man had won it. "That's what kind of guy he was."

Suggs also beat the legendary Ben Hogan one time. "His friends teased him," Louise says. "They asked him how come he wasn't wearing a skirt."

Louise Suggs (left) congratulates amateur Polly Riley after Riley beat her to win the first women's professional tournament—the Tampa Open in 1950. At right, co-sponsors Irvin Vogel (left) and Alvin Handmacher congratulate Louise Suggs after she won the 1953 Weathervane Tournament.

The face of women's golf was changing. How Glenna Collett Vare (she married Edwin H. Vare, Jr. in 1931) must have savored those Suggs victories over the men, something she had dismissed in the 1920s as being virtually impossible because of the strength discrepancy. She received firsthand knowledge of how powerful the ladies were becoming when she played in the Women's National Amateur Championship in 1947, twelve years after she had last won it. One of her matches was against Louise Suggs, who went on to win that year. The two had competed one other time, when Suggs was eighteen. Vare had beaten the youngster, one up. At the National, Suggs got her revenge.

"Where competitive golf was concerned, Glenna was a woman of few and tough words," Suggs recalls of the great champion. "She grew up in a man's world. She liked her martinis, and she was quick of tongue and play, an intimidator. During the break in the National in 1947, she stuck her head into my

Babe Zaharias illustrates the strokes she must make up to beat Louise Suggs in the 1949 Women's Open. At right, Suggs shows PGA great Sam Snead how much one of her putts fell short at the Women's Open in 1952.

room. I said to her, 'Mrs. Vare, you first won this tournament in 1923.' She said, 'Actually it was 1922—the year before you were born.' And she left."

With the first Weathervane Tournament behind him, Fred Corcoran couldn't wait to take his LPGA players overseas. At the time, the LPGA was a small but dedicated group. They had to play for pride and love of the game because there was little money. Like all pioneers, they were a collection of strong individuals rallying around a mutually held conviction. Sleeping in cheap motels, marking the courses, running tournaments, doing the dishes, and changing their own tires didn't bother them as long as they could compete on the golf course. Their adversity united them in a sisterhood. They were on a mission, bound together with the coarse strands of adversity and dedication.

While lining up a match with England's best women amateurs, Fred Corcoran found himself bragging to a British golf writer that his esteemed ladies could beat any team of British male amateurs. The moment the words were out of his mouth, he could have bitten his tongue. But it was too late. The gauntlet had been thrown down—and picked up. Corcoran obviously had a dim view of British male amateurs ("strictly weekend golfers"), and as he wrote, "In Britain, women are tolerated, not worshiped. Believe it or not, I've seen a sign on one British golf course that read: Dogs and women not allowed." He knew his hasty claim had created a no-win situation.

As predicted, his top six Weathervane finishers (Babe Zaharias, Betty Jameson, Peggy Kirk (Bell), Betty Bush, Patty Berg, and Betsy Rawls) skunked a team of former Walker Cup men, six matches to none, and not from the ladies tees. A few weeks later, the LPGA stalwarts repeated the thrashing on a group of British Curtis Cup women, 9–0. There had been individual American victories overseas, namely Babe Zaharias's (1947) and Louise Suggs's (1948) back-to-back wins of the Ladies' British Open. But the Weathervane group was America's first women's professional team, and their proficiency left no doubt in British minds that America's women golfers had caught up.

Weathervane sponsored several other transcontinental tournaments. But

contracts, and fulfilling sponsor obligations is currently handled by a staff of around sixty busy people at LPGA headquarters in Daytona, Fla. Now each tournament has its own director. But in the 1950s, even without the complication of television production, the job required the full attention of a savvy businessperson. The brief tenures logged by the string of people who tried to fill Fred Corcoran's shoes are testament to the complexity, scope, and frustrations the job entailed.

With a little smile, Betsy Rawls recalls that after Corcoran departed, Babe Zaharias and her husband, George, went after the job. George Zaharias had often said that women's golf was a racket, like wrestling, and should be run the same way. He and Babe got their shot at it. The records indicate that Babe was officially tournament director in 1954 for all of two months. Next came Betty Hicks, the 1941 Women's Amateur Champion, who had always been pressed into administrative duties on the tour because of her typing skills. She lasted a year. Golfers Fay Crocker and LPGA co-founder Marilynn Smith lasted four months before the women concluded that the job was too demanding for volunteers.

Bob Renner was the first professional hired after Corcoran. "He was the first to have charge of everything," Betsy Rawls says. "He was almost a commissioner, on site at tournaments every week. He lasted nearly three years and did a good job." A gentleman named Ed Carter followed Renner and was gone in a year. Then Fred Corcoran returned to the fold and directed the tour for three years until 1961, when Lenny Wirtz took the reins with authority.

The timing was right for Wirtz, a short, stocky man with boundless energy and little tolerance for nonsense. An NCAA basketball referee in his spare time, Wirtz was an executive at MacGregor Sporting Goods, whose job was working with the professional golfers on staff. Having just been sold to Brunswick, MacGregor was being moved from Cincinnati to Chicago. Riding the train into the Loop every day was not Wirtz's idea of progress, so when Wirtz was approached about the LPGA job, he was all ears. "It was quite a gamble," Wirtz said. Then he added with a chuckle, "I didn't know I wasn't going to get paid!" He soon learned that his salary would be directly proportional to the tournaments he initiated and the sponsors he recruited.

As president of the LPGA at the time (a position always held by a player) Betsy Rawls was one of the golfers who actively recruited Wirtz. "He brought order, structure to the LPGA," she says of the man who established rules and guidelines that were ten years overdue. "There were no regulations when I arrived, no nothing," says Wirtz, who sounds like he's still got a whistle around his

Betty Hicks Newell, 1941 Women's National Amateur Champion, apprenticed to a local male professional to qualify as the first female professional.

neck. "I wrote a constitution and bylaws. For years they had been playing with incredible liability. We got liability insurance, instituted a medical program and a retirement program. I set up dress codes, behavior codes, deadlines for signing up for tournaments, rules about bringing pets to tournaments, rules about cussing and throwing clubs—whatever came up. My credo was 'you're ladies first, golfers second.' We were all guests at these clubs, after all. I established fines. Fines for cussing out loud. Muttering was okay. Fines for throwing clubs or breaking the turf by slamming a club. If you tossed your club to a caddie and he didn't catch it, that was a fine. First offense, $25. Second offense, $50. And so on. Club throwing was the biggest problem. My rule was, I fine you, you don't pay, you don't play. I figured I'd find their choking point. When the fines started to hurt, they'd quit doing it. And I had the final vote on everything. I didn't think any player should make a decision about any other player. I was the fall guy, the bastard. That was the best way."

One thing Wirtz did have when he took over in 1961 was a cadre of great golfers. Their leader, and one of the best who ever played the game—according to champions like Ben Hogan, Gary Player, and Kathy Whitworth, to name just a few—was Mickey Wright. Whenever Wright's name is mentioned to someone who has played with her, the sweetness of her swing is the first thing they talk about. In fact Ben Hogan once said that Mickey Wright had the best swing of any woman *or* man he'd ever seen. For all of the first four years Lenny Wirtz was on the job, Mickey Wright was the tour leader and winner of the Vare Trophy (awarded for lowest average score for the season). The year before Wirtz arrived (1960), Wright had finished second and also won the Vare Trophy. During those five years she won fifty tournaments. And she was more than a great golfer.

"Everything I did hurt her," Wirtz says. "When I arrived, the winner of a tournament was getting 20 percent of the purse. There wasn't enough money left to develop new players. There had to be more money places at the bottom. I told her I intended to cut the winner's share back to 15 percent. I told her if she was going to be upset about it, she should tell me to my face. She looked me

Lenny Wirtz gave up his NCAA referee's stripes to become LPGA commissioner in 1961. Mickey Wright (right) was the habitual LPGA Tour leader during Wirtz's term.

in the eye and asked me if I thought what I was doing was in the best interest of the tour. I said yes, I thought it was. Then do it, she said.

"Mickey was incredible. If she broke a rule, no one had to turn her in. She'd fine herself. But she's a complicated person. She was so good she had to play not to lose because the news media expected her to win. If she didn't show up they got on her case. And she's one of those girls who wasn't all that happy playing on the tour, but if she were home, she'd be dying to be playing. She loved to fish. She used to meet me at 5 A.M. on the day of a tournament, and we'd go fishing for a few hours. She loves fishing, and she's good at it. She's good at whatever she puts her mind to."

Once when Wright was talking about leaving the tour after a tournament

in Midland, Tex., Wirtz told her she couldn't quit until she had broken Patty Berg's record score of 64 (for eighteen holes). Wirtz had to miss that tournament because of business meetings. That night she called him. "She told me she could quit in peace. She'd just shot a 62. I said wha'd you do, quit after sixteen holes? But it was for real. She did it again a few years later." (Se Ri Pak / 1998, and Annika Sorenstam / 1999, are the current record holders with rounds of 61. Wright's record lasted twenty years before her 62 was equaled by Vicki Fergon in 1984. Laura Davies, Hollis Stacy, Kathryn Marshall, Kristi Albers, and Meg Mallon would also shoot 62s before that mark was eclipsed.)

Today, Mickey Wright lives by herself in Port Lucie, Fla., in a house adjacent to a golf course. She rarely appears at tournaments or testimonials. But she still enjoys hitting balls, and several mornings a month she goes out when the dew is still on the grass and plays a round. Betsy Rawls says she only uses one club, a six-iron. And with that one club she generally scores around 75.

Not all the players liked the way Lenny Wirtz brought order to the LPGA chaos or his guarantee to sponsors that he would have twenty-five of the top thirty players at every tournament. But in the nine years he was tournament director, there was never any question about his full support of the women. Once Wirtz called off a tournament in San Diego during a Santa Ana wind because it was too hot on the course (the sponsors agreed). Never was his commitment more evident than when a couple of real estate sponsors tried to ban two African-American players from tournaments. One was Althea Gibson, who joined the LPGA in 1963 after a stellar tennis career. Wirtz's position was loud and clear, as usual. "We all play, or we all stay away." His stand cost the LPGA a couple of southern tournaments at a time when tournaments were precious entities. But the players stood firmly beside Wirtz on the issue.

Wirtz and women's professional golf parted ways in 1969. He does continue to follow the LPGA during his retirement in Florida. "What gets me," Wirtz says, "is that the women in today's LPGA field have no idea what the older players went through."

After a stellar tennis career, Althea Gibson became the first African-American to join the LPGA (1963). She played fourteen years without a win, but had several top-ten finishes.

FAIRWAY FASHION

"I didn't want to dress like a man.
It wasn't so much that I wanted to
get noticed. I just wanted to look
nice and look like a woman."

LAURA BAUGH

CONVENTION HAS LONG PRE-
vailed over comfort for women's golf fashion. When
women first began playing golf in America in the late
1800s, Victorian decorum demanded that women be covered from head to toe with a variety of weighty, unwieldy
garments. Because the golf links were public and convention ruled, women who played golf in those days looked
like they were dressed for late afternoon tea. Long-sleeved,
high-necked blouses were covered by heavy woolen
waistcoats and matching skirts to the floor. How any of
these women golfers could walk even a few holes in their
high-button shoes is a mystery. And that their straw
boaters, piled high with feathers and fluff, stayed on when
they swung a club is testament to their facility with pins.
How they must have suffered in the summer heat rising
from open fairways.

By the early 1900s, the skirts had risen slightly off the floor, the boaters had been replaced by berets, and the shoes were more sensible. In fact, one lady golfer was quite pleased with her more casual costume. In a newspaper article circa 1915, Mrs. Arthur B. Turnure of New York, a well-known amateur, wrote that women's attire for golf was actually an important advantage: "One may wear without inconvenience the conventional skirt. An ordinary shirt-waist, a belt, a skirt coming about to the ankles, and light but strong shoes with ties answer every requirement of conventionality and fashion in golf."

By the 1920s, the hem of the "conventional skirt"

had risen a few more inches, but the skirts seen on the links were still copious garments. They were often extra full, or pleated to accommodate the wide stance required by certain golf shots. The cloche hats followed the day's fashion. Blouses were buttoned to the neck, collars were often secured with neckties, and long sleeves were a must. So were long stockings. And the shoes remained, for the most part, cruel.

What is amazing is how long it took for women to be liberated from the confines of their apparel. In the 1930s the cut of the garments was more in harmony with the shape of the body, but long skirts prevailed, as did neckties. More comfortable shoes and short socks made some inroads, and the more adventurous ladies tried short sleeves. In their review of the first century of women's golf in America, *Golf for Women* magazine notes this about the 1930s: "the daring duffers would even slip on slacks."

The 1940s were an extension of the 1930s when it came to golf fashion, with the occasional set of plus-fours seen on the links. It wasn't until the mid-1950s that more sensible shorts finally replaced skirts. They were long Bermuda shorts of course, and the accompanying knee socks were expected, but at least the pesky full skirt would no longer fly in the wind and interfere with the arc of the club. Even in the 1950s, shorts were a hard sell. Betsy Rawls, who was on Wilson's staff at the time, recalls that the company was dead set against its staffers wearing shorts. "But we insisted, and they gave in eventually."

Golf for Women had this to say about the 1950s: "Sleeveless blouses and polos took root at country clubs. Colors got bolder. Pedal pushers and culottes were all the rage. No self-respecting woman golfer was without her

red lipstick, all-white golf spikes with kilties, bobby socks, cat's-eye sunglasses, and knitted club covers. Hats became passé—and impossible with those beehive dos."

From its inception in 1950, the LPGA Tour had an influence on the dress code for women golfers. With the exception of free spirits like Babe Didrickson Zaharias, who liked to play in off-course clothing (sweater sets, colored blouses, fashionable shoes), the early tour was dressed down, with the majority of players opting for uni-sex khaki shorts and short-sleeved navy shirts. The tour players were admittedly a drab lot until 1970, when Laura Baugh burst on the scene. Baugh was an attractive blonde whose concept of golf fashion revolutionized the look of the women's game. She showed up in a variety of miniskirts. She wore short dresses or elephant pants that were en vogue made of a light fabric that flowed off her legs when she swung a club or walked. She liked lightweight, tight mock turtlenecks for chilly days, designer T-shirts for hot days.

"I hated the old lady fashions that most of the girls wore on the golf course," Baugh wrote in her recent auto-biographical portrait (with Steve Eubanks), *Out of the Rough.* "I didn't want to dress like a man, so we had to get creative . . . It wasn't so much that I wanted to get noticed; I just wanted to look nice and look like a woman." Baugh would ultimately design her own line of women's sportswear for David Crystal.

A few manufacturers began to see women's golf as a niche in the 1970s. Lilly of Beverly Hills, Izod, and Leon Levin (originator of the "skort") were among the first to design clothes especially for golf. By the beginning of the 1980s, there was a rush to the drawing boards. By

the 1990s, Polo, Armani, Escada, and Prada were among a huge wave of designers applying themselves to the manufacture of golf apparel. Most recently, Brooks Brothers has entered the women's golf arena. And hats were making a comeback. *Golf for Women* concluded, "The ladylike look of the forties and fifties is back in vogue, with capris, skirts, and dresses gracing the fairways."

Gracing the public fairways, at least. In many private clubs, committees of men dictate what women can wear, and if it isn't shorts cut just above the knee and conservatively collared shirts, they will be asked to change. Dress code restrictions still prevail on many courses. Men also remain gripped in tradition: PGA players are not allowed to wear shorts on tour.

5 STARDOM

IN THE 1970S, THE LPGA WAS MAKING SLOW BUT steady progress. Some extremely talented golfers had begun to challenge Hall of Famers Mickey Wright and Kathy Whitworth, the dominant forces through the 1960s and 1970s with a combined 170 victories. Carol Mann, JoAnne Carner, Judy Rankin, Jane Blalock, Sandra Palmer, and Amy Alcott were just a few of the formidable female players attracted to the professional game. By the end of the 1960s, LPGA tournament money had grown to $600,000 (an increase of $420,000 in ten years). But that was the total combined purse for thirty-four events, or roughly $17,500 per event. With the winner's share averaging around $4,500, it was a tough way to make a living, even with sponsorships. Lenny Wirtz had done wonders for the internal organization, but the players were still doing all the administrative work, laying out courses, deciding the pairings, setting the pins, and making lunch. And amateurs were still being recruited to round out the field for most tournaments.

"You can't believe how uneventful it was," says Missy Eldridge, who played in an LPGA tournament in 1972 when she was just thirteen years old. Eldridge is now an LPGA Teaching and Club Professional at the Lemon Bay Golf Club in Edgewater, Fla. "It was no big deal at all. The tournaments weren't as well run as the national junior tournaments. I'd say they were second to the state tournaments. It was low-level stuff on a rundown course. The players did everything. Kathy Whitworth probably tucked me in at night."

The LPGA was in need of a boost that would launch them into the mainstream of American sports. In the 1970s, that meant television time. Without

Nancy Lopez signs autographs for fans in 1978. Often besieged by autograph seekers when outside course boundaries, Lopez always obliges.

a television deal, the bigger paydays would never arrive. The LPGA's first tele-vised tournament (the U.S. Women's Open) had been in 1963, and "Shell's Wonderful World of Golf" had included a few women's matches. Very few. The LPGA and television just weren't coming together.

Meanwhile, in the boardroom of the Colgate-Palmolive Company in Manhattan, CEO David Foster was puzzled about how to interest younger women in his company's products. An Englishman by birth, Foster was not an average CEO. He personally pounded the pavement, participating in a certain amount of door-to-door research. Colgate was more than a job for Foster. His father, William Foster—the youngest British athlete ever to win an Olympic gold medal (1908, London, 4 x 200 meter swim relay, at age eighteen)—had founded the Palmolive Soap Company in England that had merged with Colgate in 1939. Initially leery about working for his father, David Foster grew to love the business and worked himself into the top job over a twenty-year period.

In 1971, Foster was aware that while women of older generations were enthusiastic users of Colgate toothpaste, Ajax (the foaming cleanser), and Fab detergent for clothes, those products weren't being bought by younger housewives and working women. At a meeting in New York in 1971, Colgate's public relations officer, Spencer Valmy, suggested underwriting women's sports on television, golf in particular. A lifelong golfer himself, Foster immediately embraced the idea.

Why Valmy focused on women's golf is a mystery. It could have been the notoriety of Laura Baugh. The fact that Baugh won the 1971 U.S. Women's Amateur Championship when she was only sixteen years old—she remains the youngest winner of that event—was remarkable. But the fact that she was as physically appealing as she was talented created a sensation in the media. The petite blonde with the movie-star looks was a departure from the image pro-jected by the past twenty years of women professional golfers. Baugh also shunned the drab khaki and navy blue apparel of her golfing sisterhood. Whether clad in miniskirt, shorts, or slacks, Baugh shamelessly brought her flair for fashion to the links. Predictably, the media went bonkers over Laura Baugh, tabbing her a sex

Youngest ever to win the U.S. Women's Amateur Champion-ship (at sixteen), Laura Baugh brought beauty and style to golf when she turned pro in 1973.

symbol out to revolutionize women's golf: "a bombshell," "Golf's Golden Girl," "The Charlie's Angel of Golf." Even those players who were bothered by all the fuss that was made over Laura Baugh's looks knew the attention would be good for the LPGA. Alas, the bright promise of Baugh's LPGA career never came to fruition. She would fail to win a single tournament (she finished second ten times). But her initial value as a drawing card to the sport was monumental.

Colgate-Palmolive got into golf in a big way. "We compared the men's and women's golf scenes," Foster recalls, "and there *was* no comparison. We did the research and decided that if we went with the idea, we had to first of all put

the women's tournaments on a par with the men's. In 1971, the average men's tournament was worth $110,000, with a top prize of $20,000. We said okay, we'll start with that."

Foster worked fast. He realized there was already a full LPGA tournament schedule in Florida, so he began looking in California for a Colgate-Palmolive tournament venue, without much success. At the same time, he began talking with the major networks about his plan to sponsor a women's tournament. Colgate was a major television advertiser in the 1970s, but even with that clout behind him, Foster failed to interest the big three (ABC, CBS, NBC) networks. Women's golf was that hard to sell. The third key was lining up a host. The male tournaments all had celebrity hosts—from Bing Crosby and Bob Hope to Sammy Davis, Jr.—and Foster liked the effect. Moreover, he had a wonderful candidate for host, or hostess, already in the wings. For several years, Colgate had been the sponsor of a weekday morning talk show called, "Dinah's Place," starring Dinah Shore, singer-turned-TV host, whom a Gallup Poll of the early 1960s had found to be one of the most-admired women in the world. The trouble was, Dinah Shore played tennis.

"I went to see Dinah," Foster recalls. "I told her I had sponsoring a tournament in mind. 'Oh,' she said, 'tennis?' No, I told her, golf. She said, 'I'll take up golf!' And she did."

The other pieces came together. The Hughes Sports Network went for Foster's presentation, and after striking out at well-known clubs like Palm Springs' Indian Wells and Bermuda Dunes, he accepted an invitation from a newly opened golf and condo development in the desert called Mission Hills. In an effort to make the tournament as classy as possible, Foster set high eligibility standards. Only those who had won a tournament within the last ten years, those who finished second or third in a tournament in the previous three years, or LPGA Hall of Fame members could qualify. The LPGA Hall of Fame had been established in 1967. Instead of being elected, players had to earn their way in with a demanding combination of regular and major tournament victories.

David Foster, former Colgate-Palmolive CEO and champion of women's professional golf, with Dinah Shore, his "Winners Circle" tournament hostess.

Those in the Hall of Fame in 1972 were: Patty Berg, Betty Jameson, Louise Suggs, the late Babe Zaharias, Betsy Rawls, and Mickey Wright.

Foster chose the week of April 10, 1972, for his first Dinah Shore-Colgate Winner's Circle tournament because it was the week before the Masters would be played nearby. His plan to get the best golf writers to Palm Springs early to enjoy a week in the sun with their wives (gratis, of course) worked like a charm. With myriad details attended to with similar creative care, Colgate's tournament was a hit. Hughes reported a television rating of 7.6, twice that of any previously televised women's tournament, and the broadcast ranked ninth of all televised golf tournaments that year. Celebrities turned out in droves for the Pro-Am round (Bob and Dolores Hope, Frank and the future Mrs. Sinatra, Barbara Marx, Glen Campbell, Jack Benny, Joey Bishop, Rita Hayworth, Burt Lancaster, Robert Stack, among others). Janie Blalock took home $20,000, the largest cash prize ever won by a female golfer, and a car.

David Foster was ecstatic. Before the golf carts had fully recharged, he was planning the second Winner's Circle. The first thing he did was upgrade from a fifty-four-hole to a seventy-two-hole tournament. "The fifty-four-hole thing for women was ridiculous," Foster says. "The women are as strong and as willing to play seventy-two holes as any man." Having seen the results, ABC television quickly came on board. But the other networks were reluctant to run commercials urging viewers to watch an event on rival ABC. Foster had a plan for getting around that: Let the LPGA women star in the commercials. The ad agencies balked, but at Foster's insistence, they tested commercials using agency talent against the same spots using the professional golfers. There was little difference. Soon, Judy Rankin was the spokeswoman for Fab detergent; Betsy Cullen was touting the power of Ajax; ads for Cold Power detergent and Curad "ouchless" bandages featured Jan Stephenson; Betsy Rawls extolled the virtues of furniture polish; Pam Barnett got a Cleo award for her Palmolive soap spots; Marlene Hagge appeared in Baggie commercials; and Laura Baugh was another Cleo winner as the "How's your love life?" Ultra-Brite toothpaste girl. Thirty-

Picturesque Mission Hills in the California desert, where the "Winner's Circle" debuted in 1972. Janie Blalock (right) won the first tournament.

five LPGA golfers appeared in commercials for Colgate products, gaining recognition and earning residuals whenever a spot aired. The ladies were also frequent guests on NBC's "Dinah's Place," where they gave putting demonstrations, helped Dinah with cooking chores, and promoted their tournaments.

As planning for the third Winners Circle (1974) began, Foster decided to expand the program and include a Colgate-sponsored event in England. He envisioned a tournament that would feature the best British women amateurs and professionals challenging the best American professionals. This would follow the Winners Circle in 1974. He chose Sunningdale, his old course outside London, but he wasn't certain the club would approve. To test the waters, he sent a team of four professionals to Sunningdale. They played with some of the members, including Sean Connery, and the ice was broken. Once again, it was Foster's attention to advance work and details that made the event a success. He opted for BBC's non-

commercial coverage because of its 100 percent reach into British homes. He put the Colgate logo on the caddies' back cloths, correctly surmising that the cameras couldn't help but include it in shots. He invited several Sunningdale members and British golf writers and their wives to play in the Winner's Circle Pro-Am. And because he was thinking ahead to a Colgate tournament in Melbourne, Australia, Foster extended similar invitations to Australian golf writers and members of the Victoria Golf Club, and their wives. More advance work.

The 1973 Winner's Circle broke all records for attendance and TV coverage. And Sunningdale was also a wild success. "I can remember the looks of incredulousness among the gallery when our JoAnne Carner put her second shot on the green at the first hole," Foster says.

"David Foster got us where we are today," says Kathy Whitworth, who turned pro in 1958, and who knew the rigors of LPGA life before Colgate. In 1965 Whitworth had been the leading money winner with $28,658, a sum that represented eight tournament wins. "Colgate's involvement took us to a whole new level," Whitworth says. "And Foster made sure it was successful. Under his direction, Colgate bought RAM (equipment manufacturers), Etonic Shoes, a golf course in Italy . . . he created a golf empire, and we were the beneficiaries. It was a wonderful time in the history of women's golf. After England, Colgate underwrote tournaments all over the world—Hong Kong, Australia, Manilla, Malaysia. . . . And it was first class all the way, from plane reservations to hotels and restaurants. If any man should ever be made an honorary member of the LPGA Hall of Fame, it's David Foster."

Cynthia Anzolut, whose rookie year as a pro was 1959, was president of the LPGA in 1972. Anzolut signed the first contract with Colgate and David Foster. "That wasn't our first hundred-thousand-dollar contract," Anzolut says. "We had a previous deal with Sears Roebuck called the Wonderful World of Women. But David Foster took it several steps further. He pulled it all together with the TV contracts, the year-round promotions, getting players involved in commercials . . . he made stars out of them. And he was so low-key. He called the tournament the Dinah Shore–Colgate Winner's Circle. I told him he should reverse it. He was paying for it, after all. And he was so personally involved. If some player was having trouble with her clubs, he'd come out of a board meeting to talk with her."

As far as Foster was concerned, everything worked like a charm. He thoroughly enjoyed his association with the sport. The high-end approach to the tournaments put a shine on Colgate's corporate image. The effect on targeted Colgate products was very positive. And, as Foster says, it made friends and influenced people for Colgate *and* the LPGA. Arnold Palmer and Dinah Shore became pals, and when Palmer started praising women's golf, other male golfers followed suit. "Dinah ended up with a 14 handicap," Foster says. "She became a

Hall of Famers (from left): JoAnne Carner, an habitual winner from 1970 to 1984; Kathy Whitworth, whose eighty-eight LPGA wins are a record; and Amy Alcott, who finished in the top ten for nine consecutive years.

great friend. She had ideas. She lived the whole project. The players loved her. After Hall of Famer Amy Alcott won the tournament at Mission Hills in 1988, she and Dinah grabbed hands and jumped into the lake at the eighteenth hole. That started a tradition that carries on to this day."

David Foster retired from Colgate in 1979. Those who replaced him at the company had been contemplating with growing displeasure the time, money, and energy Colgate was expending on women's golf. New management voted to discontinue sponsorship of the Dinah Shore Tournament. Nabisco picked up the Tournament in 1981 and has held on tightly ever since. Foster says Colgate would have gotten rid of the tournament in 1979, but the contract he had signed with ABC lasted until 1981. And the Dinah Shore Tournament was just a portion of the sports-direction Foster took at Colgate. By the time he retired, Foster had been responsible for Colgate's purchase of fourteen companies, most of them manufacturers of sporting goods. When a British billionaire threatened the company's new management with a takeover of their sports group, they decided to divest themselves of the Foster legacy and get back to the main business of household products. But it had been an excellent run for David Foster, and for women's golf. As he says, "It all started with the LPGA."

Ray Volpe remembers Foster. Volpe became the LPGA's first official commissioner during the Colgate heyday. Formerly vice president of marketing for the National Hockey League, Volpe was amazed that Colgate wasn't paying a fee to the LPGA for broadcast rights. "I went to see Foster at the Colgate corporate offices. It was intimidating. You had to go through about forty people before you got to him at the big desk. I suggested we set the rights fee at $50,000, and he agreed. He knew it was the correct thing to do. Foster was the strength behind that whole deal. He told the truth, worked hard. He loved women and golf. He took nothing from anyone. He was as important at that time as Nancy Lopez and Carol Mann."

It was Carol Mann, who as president of the LPGA, hired Volpe as commissioner in 1975. Mann was not only a great golfer, a Hall of Fame member whose thirty-eight career victories ranks ninth on the all-time victory list, she's

Hall of Famer Carol Mann shot a career-low 65 in 1968. Her record season scoring average of 72.04, set that year, stood for ten years.

also the kind of natural leader who could run a large organization. Her business savvy and political intuition are accompanied by a wry sense of humor, subtle diplomatic skills, and a passion to make things right. She also has an immense capacity for work. "Probably," she says, "it's because I was the oldest of five children. The other four were boys. I took care of my brothers." Carol Mann turned pro in 1961 after graduating from the University of North Carolina at Greensboro. The LPGA was lucky to have her in place in 1975. As it turned out, her work at the LPGA was a prelude to even bigger advances for both women and golf.

When it became evident that a change was needed in the commissioner's office, Mann hired a professor of business management and organization to analyze the LPGA and determine what skills and what *order* of skills were needed by a commissioner. Knowledge of golf was far down on the list. At the top were marketing, knowledge of television, and the ability to sell, all items that married well with the resumé of Ray Volpe, whose name had been suggested by NBA Commissioner, Larry O'Brien. Volpe had just quit the NHL. O'Brien had wanted him in the NBA, but Volpe forbid him to mention his name. "I hated basketball," Volpe says. "O'Brien said he'd given my name to the LPGA. I asked him, 'What's that?'

"I also hated golf, and women in sports," Volpe recalls today with a grin from his large and modestly appointed office at Kaleidoscope Sports and Entertainment, where he is chairman and CEO. Volpe is a quiet-spoken, amiable man who enjoys describing himself as a cigar-smoking New Yorker. His directness is a trademark. Next to his cluttered desk, a putter leans against the wall. "The first question Carol Mann asked me at my interview was what I did first thing when I got up in the morning. I told her I went to the toilet. She laughed, and I fell in love with my first woman athlete."

One of the first things Volpe discovered after becoming commissioner was that the LPGA was bankrupt. "There was no money for the rent, no money for me," he recalls. "It was a nightmare. The women said they could take up a collection. That had apparently been done before."

Mann and her party stormed Capitol Hill, making the rounds of key senators' offices with their presentation. They also had appointments with Senate Ways and Means committee chairman John Rostenkowski; the late Patricia Higgins, commissioner of Health, Education, and Welfare; and House Speaker James Wright. They ended up in the office of President Jimmy Carter. "And we won!" Mann says, the old elation bursting forth after more than twenty years. "The win was powerful because the odds were so stacked against us," she says. "What a thrill."

But the struggle for equity in women's sports wasn't over. In 1982, the powerful NCAA usurped the fledgling Alliance of Intercollegiate Athletics for Women. That effectively put men in charge of women's intercollegiate sports. Two years later, in 1984, a Supreme Court decision (*Grove City College v. Bell*) limited Title IX's coverage to only those specific programs receiving federal assistance rather than to the institution as a whole. Suddenly, Title IX lost its teeth. The negative effects on women's sports programs were widely felt. Sixty-four claims of Title IX violations then before the Justice Department were suspended. Most of them related to sports discrimination based on sex.

Carol Mann retired from the LPGA Tour in 1981. In 1985, when she became president of the Women's Sports Foundation, the revival of Title IX became one of her first priorities. In her book, *The LPGA: The Unauthorized Version*, Liz Kahn speculated, "Carol Mann was more fulfilled as a catalyst for change than she was by winning the U.S. Open and being the leading money winner on the tour." In any case, the cerebral and dedicated Mann led the WSF into the fray once again, lining up with Jesse Jackson's Rainbow Coalition and other groups that descended upon Washington in a move to create positive changes along racial, sexual, and disabled lines. Again it was a tough fight, and again it was a victory. The result was the passing by Congress of the Civil Rights Restoration Act of 1987. It was a cliff-hanger to the end. President Ronald Reagan vetoed the bill. But it had enough strength and momentum for Congress to override the presidential veto. Among the CRRA's mandates was the rejuvenation of Title IX.

Today, many of the LPGA tour's 200 players are Title IX beneficiaries. That includes a large percentage of the many foreign players now on the tour, who came to America to study on golf scholarships. Probably the most famous Title IX player of them all is Juli Inkster, who put together three banner years in 1997, 1998, and 1999, with a scoring average of less than 71. In 1997, her career earnings exceeded $3 million. In 1999, she won five tournaments (including two majors), soared to more than $5 million in career earnings, and played herself into the Hall of Fame. For Juli Inkster, it all began with a golf scholarship at San Jose State University, thanks to Title IX.

"San Jose always had a good golf program," Juli says, "but the women's golf team was the beneficiary of the university's need to match the money spent on men's sports. There weren't that many other women's sports at San Jose, so golf got the money. Golf was able to increase its scholarship and travel budgets. Title IX had a dominant effect on women's sports. It enabled me to play against the very best players out there."

In her sixteen years in the LPGA, Inkster had recorded a few good and bad seasons scattered among a string of average performances until 1997 came along. Suddenly, this mother of two, fast approaching forty, hit her stride. "I figured out I wasn't finishing my tournaments," she said. "I looked at the situation and realized I was missing opportunities to win. So I started playing more aggressively on Sundays. My confidence grew, and I won more."

Inkster's accomplishment has sent a ripple through the world of women's sports and has been an inspiration to women in general. "I think I have showed women that they can have a career *and* raise a family," Inkster says. "You can't do it without a lot of support at home. I have a great husband, and we share responsibility for the children on a fifty-fifty basis. This is a great time for being a woman. We're starting to see prom queens in high schools and colleges who are athletes. Twenty years ago that wouldn't have happened. Sports is hard work, but it's wonderful for building self-confidence, and learning about teamwork."

The other event that had a major impact on women's golf in the 1970s

Three views of Hall of Famer Juli Inkster, a forty-year-old mother of two who began tearing up the LPGA circuit during her seventeenth year as a pro.

came two years into Ray Volpe's term as commissioner. That was in 1977, when Nancy Lopez joined the LPGA. Lopez is an appealing woman from the south-west who started playing golf with her father when she was eight years old. A golf prodigy, when she was nine she won a peewee tournament by 110 strokes. At the age of twelve, Lopez won the New Mexico Women's Amateur Championship. For all that, she might not have been allowed to play in high school if not for a woman ACLU attorney who asked the Lopez family for permission to petition the Board of Education to allow Nancy to play on the boy's golf team. (There was no girl's team, and Title IX had not been written yet.) "They had a rule against girls playing contact sports," Nancy Lopez says, "and they had extended

length of a 6,000-yard course. And instead of being stuck out in front of the standard tee boxes as an afterthought, they are integrated into the overall design of the course.

"All golf course architects have followed our lead in shrinking the yardage of courses for women," Dye says. "They have to. There are so many women playing now that their collective strength is huge. Women golfers are needed economically. Courses are so expensive to maintain that if the course isn't played all week, the books won't balance. There used to be jokes about women on the golf course. Not anymore. It's economics. Underneath every social change you usually find an economic reason."

Dye credits the golf cart's arrival on the scene with keeping women over fifty playing golf. "They aren't as strong or as athletic as they used to be, but they love to play. The cart allows them to get around the long walk."

In 1998, Alice Dye became the first and only female member of the PGA Board of Directors. "There are fourteeen men and me," Alice Dye says. "This is very new. It's part of the evolvement of our society."

SOUTHERN PINES, NORTH CAROLINA The third hole at the Donald Ross-designed Pine Needles. In 1949, Peggy Kirk won the Titleholders Championship. The following year she played on the Curtis Cup Team. Three years later she married Warren Bell and purchased the Pine Needles resort. Her golf school there is now attended by more then 1,200 women a year. The 1994 U.S. Women's Open was hosted by Pine Needles, and will be played there again in 2001.

PINE NEEDLES

Wilson-Foley had women golfers in mind from the outset, hence the name. She wanted to call the course Blue Fox. She added "run," she says with a laugh, "to keep it from sounding like a neon strip joint. But I like the 'fox' idea because it sounds sexy. I want everyone to know this is a female-friendly place."

Wilson-Foley had to negotiate with a consortium of seven Italian men in their seventies to buy the golf course. "One of their sons was the pro," Lisa says. "He was very intimidating. And of course none of the owners took me seriously. I had to ask my husband to step in and do the male thing. When they realized I actually had the money, their attitude changed. Suddenly they switched to being my grandfathers. I gave them all life memberships as part of the deal. They all play for free here."

She also hired a woman professional. "Women learn differently from men," Wilson-Foley says. "And they learn best from women. If they're going to embarrass themselves, they'd rather not do it in front of the opposite sex. Women take a lot more lessons than men, perhaps because it takes women longer to learn the game. Women are beginners for about five years. It's easy to get discouraged. A good woman professional helps."

Despite the calculated appeal to women, Blue Fox Run's clientele is 70 percent men. But Lisa has more incentives up her sleeve. She thinks golf apparel leaves much to be desired. "Women are stuck with horrible clothes," she says. "Tennis clothes are pretty good. But golf clothes are bad. Colors are important to women. If you feel good in black, why not wear it on the golf course?" Wilson-Foley is sure to get involved in golf apparel at some point, just as she plans a line of golf clubs. "It occurred to me the other day that I am playing with a club called 'Big Bertha.' Why do I have *that* club in my bag? The name is degrading to women. I want to name a club after the guy who dumped me in junior high school. Or how about 'Big Ben,' or 'Fat Freddie.'" Lisa laughs. She'll call her line of clubs Blue Fox, of course, and in addition to catchy names she wants more colors in the bag, too.

Lisa Wilson-Foley is having fun with her golf course. The women who play there, who bring their children to the day-care center and take lessons with the

Lisa Wilson-Foley is the owner of Blue Fox Run in Connecticut, a golf facility she designed with women in mind. Behind her is an enclosed play area for children at Blue Fox.

woman professional, are responding to the friendly atmosphere and the customized hospitality. Those who study the business of the sport say that among the main reasons women drop out of golf is the lack of same-sex playing partners. Clubs like Blue Fox Run will help solve that problem, even though it's not one that Lisa Wilson-Foley personally shares. "I want to play with men," she says. "I play better with men, and I want to do business with them. I want to connect like the guys connect. I want to get to know my business associates better. I believe you should have a relationship with someone before you sign a contract with him."

Sentiments like that are music to the ears of Suzanne Woo, an attorney who now teaches women (mostly) how to use golf as a business tool. Her company, BizGolfDynamics.com is located in Berkeley, Calif. Woo started to play golf

when she decided to specialize in real estate land-use law and realized her client base would be affluent men. She thought it would be advantageous to connect with them in some other way besides the law. So she took up golf, worked at it, and soon had a handicap in the teens. "Other women I met were astonished that I played and was getting to know my clients on the golf course. So I saw a need to teach women how to leverage a golf course," Woo says, dropping comfortably into pop-business speak. "I developed seminars for women's groups. It grew into a full-time occupation." Men sometimes attend her seminars, but she says when men are present it shifts the atmosphere. "It goes back to those days in the sixth grade," she says. "The men do all the talking, and the women clam up."

Woo doesn't teach golf. Her emphasis is on golf etiquette and rules. "You can be confident on the golf course even if you don't have a great swing," Woo says, "by knowing how to handle yourself, by knowing the rules— especially the local rules—the terminology, and by steeping yourself in the culture of the game. New players are like foreigners in a strange country. How do you improve that situation? Get a guidebook. It's the same on the golf course. Knowing the rules and the etiquette of golf, sensing when to pick up your ball if you're taking too many shots, helping others look for balls, knowing not to step on someone's line on the green—all those things can make you a better partner than some good golfer who is unpleasant on the course.

"And golf is 46 percent putting. You can practice that at home or at the office. I tell women to bring their putters to the office, let co-workers know you play so you'll get invited. You may not be a star on the tee, but you'll be a star on the green if you start sinking those ten-footers. Like the old saying goes, drive for show, putt for dough."

Woo doesn't advocate using a game of golf to talk business. But for those who must, she has a plan. "Use holes one through six to get to know the person. Talk business if you must on seven through thirteen. Then use fourteen through eighteen for trust-building." But for Woo, working on the relationship is the long-term value. "Who you see on the golf course is probably someone you'll be

Former attorney Suzanne Woo teaches women the value of golf as a business tool through her company BizGolfDynamics in Berkeley, Calif.

negotiating with," Woo says. One of her BizGolf tactics is what she calls the "stealth" round. "Get clues about the person by the way he handles himself on the course. Form a mental dossier on him so you'll know who you're dealing with."

So for the twenty-first century woman, the golf course has become her playing field, a legitimate sphere of operations sporting, social, and business. As Juli Inkster says, "It's a great time to be a woman." Especially a woman interested in golf.

Why, then, has the total number of women playing golf dipped slightly at the end of the 1990s? The National Golf Foundation, established in 1936 to foster the growth and economic vitality of golf, reports that 5.1 million women are currently participating in the sport, a figure down slightly from the 5.75 million participating as 1999 began. About 1.15 million of those were beginners. The same relative numbers exist for male golfers. More beginners of both sexes than ever before took up the game in 1999 (3.2 million) but almost as many dropped out. The golf industry calls it the "leaky bucket" syndrome. Time is obviously a major factor. Despite the recent push by golf course authorities and professional associations to speed up play, an eighteen-hole round of golf takes the better part of five hours when one includes driving time and a cold drink afterward.

Leslie Day Craige, editor-in-chief of *Golf for Women* magazine, says golf participation for both sexes has peaks and valleys. "Any sport goes through a period of popularity because of a 'Lopez effect,' or a 'Tiger effect,'" she says, "when both men and women enter in droves—especially young people. But for women, playing golf is more cyclical. It has to do with time commitments. A woman has more time during high school and college because her time is structured, and there are teams and leagues. Then she begins a career and stops for awhile. Women don't tend to quit golf. They just take a hiatus. They'll stop for awhile because of the birth of a child, then start playing again. The reason you see so many women seniors playing is they have the time."

Those in the women's golf business, like Leslie Day Craige, are also very aware of the lingering sexism and discrimination that inhibits the growth of their sport.

Leslie Day Craige keeps tabs on form, fitness, fashion, philosophy, and the future, as editor in chief of twelve-year-old *Golf for Women* magazine.

ter to the way the female professionals play than to the power game of the male professionals. And once they are exposed to it, once they give it a chance, they become advocates. In this world you can't compare women's sports with men's sports. The PGA will always have bigger purses. Compare women's sports with other women's sports. If you do that, the LPGA is close to the top."

Never have there been so many women playing so well at the top of professional golf. Thanks to the amount of media coverage they are getting and their celebrity presence in advertising campaigns, their names are becoming familiar: Webb, Inkster, Mallon, Davies, the Sorenstams, Pepper, Pak, Kim, just to mention a few. The top women frequently score in the 60s. Many of them average 250 yards or more off the tees. Average! Remarkable. As Charlie Mechem says, watching them play is a joy. Their swings are a study in rhythm and timing. Their control is amazing. As it always has been, the players in the forefront of women's golf set the pace for female players across the country. They share their secrets in print and with instructional videos. They put their

expertise and experience into consulting on apparel and equipment. Collectively, their influence is casting a wider net in the ever-advancing world of women's golf. As a result, the challenge and joy of competition is a bigger drawing card for women's golf than ever before. For women, golf is competition, golf is a romp. Golf is social, golf is business. Golf is a brisk five-hour walk in a sylvan setting interrupted by ninety seconds of hitting a ball. Golf is an escape from the frenzy of business, the routine of housework, the responsibility of children.

The lesser lights burn just as steadily, if not as brightly. A woman in Florida who found the solitude of the golf course a welcome refuge in the confusing social turmoil of her teenage years, developed into an excellent amateur in her twenties. Now in her fifties, she is a perennial club champion. She still sneaks off for nine holes by herself when she can.

When asked what she likes best about the game that has held her attention for nearly fifty years, a seventy-year-old woman in Massachusetts confessed with a smile that for her, driving the golf cart around the course is the most fun. Slightly crippled from a childhood bout with polio, this woman uses her club as a cane until she gets to the ball, then takes a full swing. This woman's daughter, in her forties, has almost as much fun finding the lost balls of other golfers as she does playing. They both play creditable games, and golf is their favorite mother-daughter pastime.

Craige's late grandmother played regularly with her husband (a club champion) from the 1940s on. When her husband died, golf became her life. Craige says she quickly learned it was useless to visit her grandmother on a Sunday when the LPGA was on television.

And a middle-aged woman from Detroit travels all over the country with her retired husband in their van with two bags of golf clubs. Their idea of a perfect two-week trip is to play ten or more different golf courses.

Women love golf for many reasons, but perhaps Glenna Collett put it best when she spoke of "the long fairway, like a flowing river caressed by sun and wind that is unrolled like a magic carpet upon which women can walk to the heights."

Sweden's Annika Sorenstam has accumulated eighteen wins in the last five years, and rankings of 1-3-1-1-4. She and Se Ri Pak share the LPGA record raw score (61) for eighteen holes.

PLAYING BY THE RULES

"When I get held up on the golf
course it's usually because men are
playing ahead of me."

—BONNIE BLAIR TYLER
Club Champion (2000)
Silver Spring Country Club, Ridgefield, Conn.

THE RULES OF GOLF "AS APPROVED
by the United States Golf Association and The Royal and
Ancient Golf Club of St. Andrews, Scotland," are substantial.
The most recent edition of *The Rules* (copyright 1999, effective January 1, 2000) is 127 pages. And unlike the official
rules for any other sport, *The Rules of Golf* includes etiquette.
In fact, the very first section of *The Rules* is titled "Etiquette," and
begins, "Prior to playing a stroke or making a practice swing,
the player should ensure that no one is standing close by or in
a position to be hit by the club, the ball, or any stones."

Women are students of the rules. But for men, *The
Rules of Golf* may be one of the most ignored books in print.
Male golfers have a surface knowledge of the rules at best.
What they do know has probably been picked up on the
course from fellow players who learned the same way.

But women have a different approach to the rules.
David Norman, executive director of the Virginia State Golf
Association and a veteran rules official, wrote a humorous
piece in *Virginia Golfer* a few years ago about how men's
and women's view of the rules of golf differ. "Ladies," Norman
wrote, "will generally make you putt out, make sure you are
not in front of the markers when you tee off, and will make you
replay from the tee with a stroke and distance penalty from a
lost ball. Men will offer a gimme for a two-foot putt (unless it's
the last hole of a match), and let you drop one at the edge of
the woods with a one-stroke penalty for a lost ball."

Norman continues: "Before teeing off, ladies always
count their clubs to make sure they don't have more than fourteen. Before teeing off, men dig into their trunks to put an
extra putter and driver or two in the bag in case 'old reliable'
isn't working that day.

"When ladies enter a tournament, it's business as
usual. When men enter a tournament, it's time to panic."

Why are women historically such sticklers? The
answer, simply, is that playing strictly by the rules exempted
women from criticism as they fought to establish their rightful
place on the links. Their struggle with gender discrimination on the golf course is well documented. In the interest
of advancing their cause, women set out to be beyond
reproach where the rules were concerned.

They also learned to play quickly. *The Rules of Golf*
Section 1, Etiquette, Pace of Play states: "In the interest of all,
players should play without delay." Far be it for a foursome of
women to create a logjam on the course. Normally women
don't take four or five practice swings before making a shot,
or agonize over putts. A National Golf Association survey has
concluded that (novices of both genders excepted) women
play golf faster than men. And their attention to the rules makes
their male counterparts look mighty nonchalant.